DATE DUE

AUG 1 8 2004			
2/06 BA			
OCT NH 2006			
NT-12-06			
5/08 WE			
AY 10/08			

SHERLOCK HOLMES AND THE LONG ACRE VAMPIRE

A death appears to have been caused by a vampire. But surely vampires do not exist. Sherlock Holmes and Dr Watson are invited to solve the mystery of this inexplicable death in the theatrical area of London's West End. As always, after a thorough investigation, Holmes is able to apprehend the culprit.

VAL ANDREWS

SHERLOCK HOLMES AND THE LONG ACRE VAMPIRE

Complete and Unabridged

LINFORD
Leicester

First published in Great Britain in 2001 by
Breese Books Limited, London

First Linford Edition
published 2003
by arrangement with
Breese Books Limited, London

British Library CIP Data

Andrews, Val
   Sherlock Holmes and the Long Acre Vampire.—
   Large print ed.—
   Linford mystery library
   1. Holmes, Sherlock (Fictitious character)—
   Fiction 2. Watson, John H. (Fictitious character)
   —Fiction 3. Detective and mystery stories
   4. Large type books
   I. Title
   823.9'14 [F]

   ISBN 0–7089–4899–5

Published by
F. A. Thorpe (Publishing)
Anstey, Leicestershire

Set by Words & Graphics Ltd.
Anstey, Leicestershire
Printed and bound in Great Britain by
T. J. International Ltd., Padstow, Cornwall

This book is printed on acid-free paper

1

Sir Henry Irving

'How would you like to see a vampire, Watson?'

Mr Sherlock Holmes was always fond of the provocative question and he asked me this one on a winter evening at 221B Baker Street toward the end of the nineteenth century. I had been staying with him at the old rooms where he still resided and which he would, in fact, occupy for another three or four years. I had enjoyed my sojourn with my friend and the sights and sounds of nostalgia; not just those of the passing parade in Baker Street itself but those actually caused by my friend. His rattling and rustling of newspapers, the notes produced upon his violin and the pouring of liquid from tube to pipette at his chemistry bench. There were nostalgic odours too, not only those produced by his chemical experiments but also from the clouds of acrid tobacco smoke generated by a variety of pipes. Then, of course, the frequent coming and going of a variety of characters, bizarre and sedate, weird and wonderful.

I answered his question. 'Having read Stoker's novel, published two or three years ago, I do not believe that I would enjoy the experience. Moreover, since these murders in the area of Long Acre I would not be too smug in my lack of belief in the existence of such creatures.'

I referred to newspaper reports, spine-chillingly dreadful, of the discovery of a body in an alley off St Martin's Lane, bearing the scars at the throat so well described by Stoker. One could believe that this murder was performed by a killer with a sharp pointed object, delivering two stabbing thrusts to his victim's throat had it not been for two other facts. The first that another body had been discovered a morning or two later within the same general area bearing identical twin punctures. The other worrying fact that both bodies appeared to have been heavily deprived of blood, indicating to the reader that both murders had been effected by some form of blood-sucking vampire! Of course, the authorities did not suggest anything of the kind but the journalists were full of avid speculation. I had assumed that Holmes referred to these amalgams of fact and fiction. However this was not the case.

'You will remember our old friend Sir Henry Irving?'

'Why yes, did you not recover his cane with the diamond-studded knob, the one presented to him at the conclusion of the run of *The Bells*?'

'That is correct, Watson and, although that was a long time ago, he has been kind enough to send me two front stalls for tonight's performance of his dramatization of *Dracula* at the Lyceum.'

'I see, so you are inviting me to see a theatrical vampire — I wondered if you referred to these Long Acre murders?'

'My profession leads me to dealing with fact rather than fiction, Watson, but I cannot deny that a theatrical performance of *Dracula* could be quite diverting. Indeed, I had wondered how long it would take for an enterprising impresario to stage such a presentation.'

I need hardly say that I too was intrigued to see how this strange novel could be staged. Remembering Irving, with his dramatic presence, personal magnetism and magnificent voice, I did not find it difficult to picture him as Count Dracula. We dined at Simpson's in the Strand, it being within strolling distance of the Lyceum, and then made our way in that direction at half-past seven, for the performance was advertised to commence at eight. We lingered between the columns outside to view the display of photographs and posters. There upon an easel stood a splendid portrait of Sir Henry, though not in make-up and costume as Dracula: rather it was a portrait which travelled everywhere with him for front-of-theatre display regardless of the piece being performed. I was reminded of his splendid features, for it was a profile which emphasized rather than modified his magnificent Roman nose. With his collar-length hair and aristocratic pose, it was easy to see that he was the original for the long-held image of an actor-manager. Irving was imitated by hundreds but equalled by none. Standing at pavement level were the smaller framed portraits of the supporting actors and actresses: Ashley Barrington, Peggy Mountjoy, Griselda Hargreaves and Charles Mornington. There were doubtless others but probably I considered they would be supernumeraries. The poster was intriguing too, with a picture of Count Dracula at the right-hand top corner. It was worded, I believe, in the following fashion:

THE LYCEUM THEATRE

DRACULA

A play based upon the
novel by Bram Stoker.

By Barry White and
Sir Henry Irving

with

HENRY IRVING
as Count Dracula

Charles Mornington
as Dr Van Helsing

Supported by
Peggy Mountjoy,

Griselda Hargreaves
and Ashley Barrington.

NIGHTLY AT 8

Prospective patrons of a
nervous disposition
are warned that there are
some tense moments.

We chuckled at the words at the bottom of the playbill and Holmes commented, 'Nothing like a warning of fear and gore to entice people into a theatre, Watson.'

But although we appreciated this touch of showmanship we were as surprised as anyone else at the sight of a number of nurses in uniform who stood in attendance in various parts of the auditorium.

Holmes chuckled as we settled into our seats. 'Sir Henry has a good feeling for *Grand Guignol*, Watson; I feel sure we are in for an enjoyably spine-chilling evening.'

I could only agree with his words and I noted with interest that there was a full pit orchestra, more usual for a musical comedy or light entertainment than a play. Moreover the musicians were attired in evening wear of an earlier day and contributed a spirited overture of a blood-tingling style, moderating to a pianissimo background accompaniment throughout the play, with the occasional intrusion in the dramatic scenes.

According to my programme the first scene, a painted front cloth showing a mountain view, was titled: 'A Mountain Road in Transylvania'. A smocked villager entered from one side of the stage and Ashley Barrington as Renfrew entered from the opposite wing. He was in a greatcoat and carrying a carpet-bag. He spoke the opening lines of the play. 'My good fellow, can you please direct me to Castle Dracula?'

The villager threw an arm in front of his face and backed away. Renfrew said, 'Of course, I had forgotten that I was in Transylvania. Perhaps you do not understand English?'

The yokel replied, 'I understand English, but Castle Dracula: nobody goes there!'

Then he made a hasty exit. The lines were chillingly delivered and there was a black-out but when the lights returned there was a full stage set, the interior of the entrance hall at Castle

Dracula. It was an impressive scene and the designer had done his best to make it one of decayed gothic splendour. At the centre back there was a door partially obscured by imitation cobwebs. To the left of it was a staircase with a railed platform at the top and a large impressive fireplace was the right-hand feature. Ghostly music was heard, very softly from the orchestra, as property bats flew across on wires and imitation rats were drawn across the boards by the same means. From where we sat these things were obvious, yet I imagined that from the gallery and the pit, where most of the critical element would be seated, it must have looked very creepy and effective. The bats and rats got 'Ooers' from the back of the theatre auditorium whilst around us there were ironic guffaws. The door at centre stage shook and one could hear someone banging upon it from the outside. Eventually it flew open to reveal Renfrew, now dusted by imitation snow and behind him the blackness of the night and the sounds of a wild wind. Renfrew entered and threw down his carpet-bag and pushed the door closed behind him with difficulty due to the wind. Then once he was safely inside with the door shut he crossed to the fireplace, extending his hands to the low flames. Then he turned and after recoiling from a swirling bat he called, softly at first but eventually more loudly when he got no reply, 'Hello, is there anyone there? Renfrew to see Count Dracula!' Then as the lights became low there was that tremor running through the audience; a mixture of the anticipation of the first entrance of the leading player and the drama of the situation. As the lighting became dimmer a spotlight focused upon the small railed platform at the top of the stairs. Like a full moon it suddenly incorporated a shadow, that of a caped shape which suddenly materialized into the actual figure of Dracula, as portrayed by Sir Henry Irving. He was in full court evening dress with tail coat and black silk knee breeches. His cape, black with a crimson lining, had a stand-up collar and a gold neck chain. His facial make-up was a mixture of the Demon King in pantomime and a distinguished orchestral conductor. The up-pointed eyebrows in stiff black, contrasted strangely with the collar-length luxuriant white hair that could only belong to an actor. The music had built up to this entrance and now it ceased as the stage lights were again raised. Irving — Sir Henry Irving, the greatest actor manager of his day — held his pose during the considerable applause which his entrance had occasioned. This lasted for nearly a minute I would estimate, and during it he did not move a muscle. As it subsided he animated his face into a demonic smile and spread his arms, making wings of his cloak. He broke the theatre rule of seemingly being aware of his audience, gazing out at them, rather than at Renfrew, whom he addressed, 'Mister Renfrew, welcome, welcome to Castle Dracula!'

He assumed a Hungarian accent and spoke his line beautifully, with a perfect projection which must have reached the Strand itself, let alone the back of the gallery. Indeed it merited another round of applause, albeit of shorter duration than that which had greeted his entrance. Then, as Renfrew responded (in a deferential style which suggested to me that he had been trained carefully not to upstage Sir Henry), the play proper began.

I am not going to describe the rest of the play for the benefit of the reader who has doubtless at some time read Bram Stoker's famous novel but I will just mention that the play-book was wrapped but loosely about the novel itself. Indeed it had been adapted and modified not just for the purposes of theatrical presentation but also in a manner which made it a perfect vehicle for Sir Henry who, a decade or so earlier, had created a theatrical legend with his famous mad scene in *The Belle's Stratagem*. Irving had clearly had made for him a perfectly fitting set of fangs which it was evident that he did not wear throughout but cunningly introduced into his mouth a few seconds prior to those moments when that combination of lunar and dramatic situation demanded. The audience gasped with horror — even the sophisticates in the stalls — as his head raised from its position poised over the neck of his victim, the fangs gleaming in the spotlight and running with theatrical blood!

At the first interval, which occurred at the point in the play where Count Dracula had displayed those famous fangs for the second time (as he raised his head from the no longer milk-white neck of the actress who played the heroine's friend), we repaired to the bar.

Sherlock Holmes lit a small cigar of the type which I believe is called a cigarillo, a sort of Mexican combination of cigar and cigarette. Indeed, I considered that his smoking tastes seemed to grow more catholic with the passing years. There were murmurs in the bar as an extremely muted newsvendor plied his wares. But despite his no doubt forbidden sales chant one could clearly see his placard which proclaimed,

THE LONG ACRE VAMPIRE
STRIKES AGAIN

I obtained a paper and studied the headline and report which appeared below it. There was a general rustling around us with most of the imbibers being anxious to read of the bizarre killing. Holmes demanded that I read the report aloud to him, and as I did so he closed his eyes and left his cigar to burn in the ashtray.

'Long Acre, a stone's throw from the Strand, was again the scene of a most gruesome and horrific murder, evidently carried out by the Vampire, as he has been popularly named.

14

The previous two Dracula murders were evidently carried out in the area in those hours of darkness when the streets are all but deserted. This latest atrocity has been carried out at a much earlier hour, though one when many people are attending the theatre, dining or disporting themselves in taverns. At about half-past seven the body of a young woman, her painted face and style of dress indicating her class and profession, was discovered in an alley just off Long Acre itself. As with the previous killings there were twin punctures at her throat, as if a fanged animal had attacked her. However, the police have informed us that as before they suspect that the toothmarks are those of a human assailant. Doubtless we will be able to give our readers more information in our late-night edition but for the moment we can only comment upon the exact similarity of the crimes and the fact that Sir Henry Irving is impersonating Count Dracula, who is Bram Stoker's blood-sucking Vampire at the Lyceum; a theatre in very close proximity to all of the crime sites. We are surprised that no mention of the coincidental circumstance has until now been stated.'

I paused and interpolated, 'One wonders how this paper with the report of a crime only discovered at half-past seven could have been produced in time for us to be reading it at (I studied my dress watch) nine?'

Holmes said, 'Indeed no moss was gathered, for the ink is still wet!'

'How can you tell that from where you sit?'

'Watson, I see the black traces upon your white dress gloves.'

At this point the bell for the impending commencement of Act Two was rung and we made our way back to our seats. Then, as the play began again, one could sense a change in the way in which the audience received it. Irving had another big entrance, carefully crafted by himself and his fellow dramatist, and again there was applause, but it was far more subdued than that of his opening appearance. *Sotto voce* I remarked upon this to Holmes who replied in equally soft tone, 'The audience are shocked by the news which has spread all over the theatre during the interval. Even the most pudding-headed of them cannot believe that Irving has any involvement, yet the play itself now reminds them that the play might not be entirely dealing with the impossible. Let us hope for Sir Henry's sake that the whole thing is soon cleared up and then quickly forgotten.'

One of the most effective and dramatic moments in the play occurred, when the sounds of howling and wailing were heard and Count Dracula declaimed, 'Children of the night, how sweetly they sing!'

Yet obviously the audience were reminded of some monster lurking in nearby Long Acre, and the line which doubtless had dramatic effect just produced an uneasy silence. There were none of those gasps of shocked pleasure that one might have expected. Then during the third act things were worse, with the odd shout of displeasure whenever Count Dracula appeared, doubtless from someone simple enough to be unable to separate Irving from the killer who had struck again so near to where they had gathered for entertainment. I was reminded of the time when in my youth I had attended the performance of a melodrama in a mummer's booth upon Hampstead Heath. Some men in the audience had actually risen from their seats and set about the actor who played the villain when during the action of the play he had raised his hand to the heroine. But that had been many years earlier and the audience a rabble paying but a penny to witness the play, and many of them drunk at that. I could not believe that similar stupidity could be entering the brains of members of a West End theatre audience!

Then, at the end, there was frenzied applause from the gallery as Von Helsing drove a stake through Count Dracula's heart, and when the calls were taken Irving got only polite applause. How could a news item change completely the attitude of the audience toward not just the piece that they were watching but also the favourite matinee idol they more usually lauded?

As we stood for the National Anthem Holmes muttered, 'I do not relish our meeting with Irving for it is to his dressing room that we must next repair.'

We were taken to Sir Henry Irving's dressing room by a subdued call boy who knocked upon the door of that apartment and announced, 'Mr Sherlock 'Olmes and 'is colleague, Dr Watson!'

Irving's rich voice, no longer delivered with the Hungarian accent, bade us enter. He shook hands with both of us warmly and caused his dresser to find some extra chairs. Then as we sat, smoking his cigars and supping his brandy, he spoke to us as he removed his Dracula disguise. 'Holmes, did you notice that atmosphere which began to pervade the theatre? The previous two crimes of this type seemed to have no effect but now I suppose there is an unwelcome feeling of coincidence. I may have to take off the play. When I invited you here tonight I, of course, had no idea that a third ghastly crime would occur, as you can imagine. I was concerned enough about the previous atrocities to want to enlist your aid. Now I am even more desperately worried that this dreadful business should be cleared up. Not just because I have a lot of capital riding upon this enterprise but because I am genuinely concerned for the victims, or rather now for their families. Despite what you have read or might have heard, I am not a wealthy man: few actors are, but I am willing to pay your fee, which I know to be most fair and practical, if you will investigate the matter for me.'

Holmes answered in soothing tones, 'Surely, Sir Henry, the police will quickly apprehend the murderer and all will be well?'

The noble thespian replied, 'Yes, but I would substitute the word 'eventually' and by the time they have nabbed the culprit I could be bankrupt. I remember how quickly and expertly you cleared up that other matter for me. People have been kind enough to refer to me as a genius but my talent has been learned by years of touring and some sacrifice; yours, however, is surely instinctive.'

Holmes was not especially flattered, saying, 'The harder I work the more 'instinctive' I become.'

I interjected, 'My dear Sir Henry, you would be amazed to see the hard work performed by my friend, also the painstaking research, not to mention the burning of the midnight oil in solving his cases.'

'I did not mean to infer that it was

easy, just that Holmes makes it appear so.'

Sherlock Holmes grunted. 'You mean when I tell you that your wife is away at the moment and that your cairn terrier is badly trained, perhaps spoilt, and that your housekeeper is dissatisfied with her situation, you believe I speak from instinct.'

The distinguished actor paused in the work of cleaning the theatrical make-up from his face and gazed at Holmes in disbelief. 'No sir, I would say that you did so through witchcraft!'

Holmes smiled and explained, 'I observe your street clothes hanging upon their pegs, and your tweed trousers are somewhat marred in appearance by a dog's hairs, those pepper and salt grizzled kind usually associated with cairns. Were your wife at home I assume she would not have permitted you to leave the house in such a state, even if she does spoil the dog and allow it to jump up and leave its hairs upon you. As for your housekeeper, she cannot be guarding her situation with you if she does not notice these details. She will probably blame the parlour maid, yet it is her own responsibility.'

Sir Henry nodded with understanding. 'In a previous age you would have been burned for being in league with the evil one. As it is you have proved your point. It is observation and logic developed though to an extraordinary degree. Please say that you will help me, my dear fellow?'

Holmes nodded kindly. 'My dear Sir Henry, of course I will give what help I can, though I can promise nothing. By the way, do we know who is handling the matter for Scotland Yard?'

'Fellow called Lestrade, Inspector Lestrade. Do you know him?'

'Yes, our paths have crossed many times. He is a splendid fellow, brave as a lion, intelligent, straight as a die; yet he is a little bit lacking when it comes to imagination. But no man other than Watson would I wish to have with me in a tight corner. Yes, George Lestrade is a good man.'

'Shall you confer with him?'

'At my earliest opportunity.'

'Can't thank you enough, Holmes. Now perhaps Dr Watson and your good self would care to take a late supper with me?'

I was rather hoping that Holmes would agree to accept this invitation, but he declined, saying, 'I feel that Watson and I might be better employed at this moment by taking a look at the scene of the tragedy near Long Acre.'

Irving said, 'I say, I imagine the police johnnies will have covered all that by now, will they not?'

Holmes grunted. 'Covered is probably the right word, but there may be a morsel left to be devoured by Sherlock Holmes!'

Irving was pleased with my friend's zeal, saying, 'By Jove, Holmes, you have lost none of your enthusiasm for your work. I picked the right man before and I am fortunate to find you just as full of energy of body and mind.'

As we left the theatre and strolled the short distance to Long Acre I remarked, 'As soon as he mentioned that late supper I suddenly felt quite peckish. Still, never mind . . . '

Holmes cut in, 'My dear Watson, I sometimes think that you just live to eat. The difference between us is that I just eat to live. Now if you cast a glance to your left you may notice some police presence, no doubt at the scene of the crime.'

I glanced to one side to see several constables forming a square around a roped-off area. They stood facing outward from this grisly place, their hands behind them and their heads inclined forward, rather like guardsmen at a royal laying in state. But as we got closer we realized that their heads were inclined more through fatigue than from respect. The site of the crime was at the corner of Neal Street and of course the body had been long removed but evidently the police considered there might still be clues to be found. Holmes spoke to one of the constables, 'PC Roberts, is it not? I remember we were both involved with the case of the disembodied head that was discovered in Westminster Abbey. My name is Sherlock Holmes.'

The portly policeman broke into a broad grin. 'Well, bust my buttons if it ain't, and blow me if you ain't got the Doctor with you. Has old Lestrade asked for your help?'

Holmes shook his head. 'Not as yet, Roberts, but I have a feeling that he may; for you must admit that this is something far more than a run-of-the-mill murder, being one of a series of similar outrages.'

'Puts you in mind of old Jack the Ripper, eh, Mr Holmes?'

'There are similarities, and yet there is no selection of any particular group in society: the three victims are unalike in most respects, are they not?'

'Well sir, the first two was very

average so to speak, but today's victim was a . . . how shall I put it . . . lady of the night . . . even if she was out and about rather early!'

'Quite so, and if the next victim should be a minister of the church we are dealing no doubt with a complete lack of selection. Time will tell, though heaven forbid that there should be another victim. Tell me, Roberts, the two throat wounds were as in the previous cases?'

'Yes sir, just like the job had been done by a bloomin' vampire. Pardon my jocularity, but I hope Sir Henry Irving has a good means of accounting for his time at about seven to half past the hour?'

I felt bound to remark, 'From eight, several hundred people could account for where he was. Before that, his dresser, the call boy, the stage manager? All of these must have been aware of his presence in the theatre, Roberts. After all, even earlier than that he could scarcely have left the theatre dressed and made up as Count Dracula?'

The policeman's manner eased. 'I was not serious, Doctor. Sir Henry is above suspicion, but a man was seen leaving the crime scene in a cape and had a rather strange appearance; just as if he had stuff on his face.'

Holmes demanded, 'Stage make-up, theatrical grease paint?'

'I did not see him, sir, but a witness did suggest something of the kind.'

I said to my friend, 'I say, Holmes, that does sound rather strange.'

He replied, 'We could be dealing with a maniac, inspired either by Irving and his play or by Stoker's novel. But certainly his choosing the close proximity of the Lyceum casts a singular aspect upon it all. Tell me, Roberts, was anything found upon the ground near the body?'

'No objects or weapons or anything like that, just some white powder.'

'Really. Has it been analysed?'

'Sure I don't know, sir, but old Lestrade did not seem to be too interested in it. However, his sergeant collected some of the powder and put it in a packet.'

Holmes enquired, 'Do you imagine there are any traces of it left? If so, perhaps you could show me where it was found.'

'Why yes, sir, there was a sort of trail of it from the murder scene and for fifty yards or so in the direction of Covent Garden Market. Then there was a small mound of it. The trail has disappeared by now through being stepped on and ridden over.'

'How about the mound?'

'There could be some left, sir. I'll show you.'

Roberts led us for some fifty yards or so up Long Acre until indeed we came upon traces of white powder which had been preserved through its proximity to the kerb. Holmes crouched and scooped up some of the powder with one of his visiting cards. We then poured it into an envelope which he placed in his pocket. Then we returned to the roped-off area and were allowed to step within this boundary. As it happened, the men from Scotland Yard had not overlooked anything that the murderer might have dropped. There were footprints, small ones and larger ones, positioned as if to indicate a struggle.

At length, Holmes announced, 'The attacker was of average build if the rest of him followed his boot size. This is not always the case, Watson, as you know. He wore dress boots, and the heel marks suggest that he may be somewhat splay-footed. Notice, Watson, that the outer edges of the heels have been repaired recently whilst the soles are just as they were when they left the boot shop.'

'You mean his wearing of the outer edges of the heels indicates a lack of even pressure? How can you tell that the soles have not been repaired?'

'They were purchased from a shop in St James's where the trademark is always imprinted on the sole. Notice the faint traces of the word 'Clifton'.'

I could see the latter imprinted in the mud but could make nothing of them until I realized that of course they would be back to front and the right way only on the sole itself.

Holmes continued, 'Clifton's do not to my knowledge supply a repair service; the cobbler would have affixed fresh soles, obliterating that trade style.'

There seemed little more to be discovered so we bade Roberts and his fellow constables a kind goodnight and made our way back to Baker Street.

2

Enter Inspector Lestrade

I feel sure that the reader will be tired by now with accounts of my tardiness in rising and taking breakfast but I am forced to say that I was late to the breakfast table on the morning following our visit to the Lyceum to see Henry Irving as Count Dracula. Sherlock Holmes spared me his irony, with his attention being giving to the morning papers. 'Watson, the English journalist is fast becoming fond of inaccurate fictionalized reports of the more sensational crimes. I would be grateful if you would read this front page *story* (as the Americans call such reports) and give me your considered opinion upon it?'

He passed to me a broadsheet titled *The Daily Fanfare* and I tried the twin tasks of reading the story he indicated and dealing with my eggs and devilled kidneys.

THE BLOODSUCKING BEAST OF LONG ACRE

The monster with a taste for human blood has struck again, for the third time within less than a week! His latest victim, an actress, Miss Glenda Joseph, was murdered in Long Acre last evening. As with the previous killings in the area the cause of death was one unknown in the annals of murderous crime. She died as a consequence of having her throat bitten and her blood being sucked from her veins. There were, as it happens, few persons abroad in the area at that time but witnesses report seeing a caped man of demonic appearance fleeing from the inert form of Miss Joseph. One declared, 'He was running, with his eyes popping nearly out of his head, and blood dripping from his mouth.' This witness did not suggest that the murderer disappeared in any supernatural sense but he said, 'One minute he was there and the next he was not!' Inspector Lestrade of Scotland Yard has told our reporter: 'I expect to make an arrest very shortly.'

'Well, what do you make of it, Watson?'

As I laid down the newspaper I said, 'The whole thing is written in a wildly exaggerated style but the only complete fiction would appear to be in the reference to the vanishing assailant.'

Holmes commented, 'One senses that even there he has covered his tracks by substituting the word 'minute' where 'second' was implied. Feeble-minded readers will forget that it would be possible for Barnum's Jumbo to be out of public gaze within sixty seconds.'

I had to admit that I had been taken

in by this trick of journalism.

At last Holmes began to tax me with my sloth, which I had known to be inevitable. 'I wish you would finish your breakfast, Watson, for you have not, as you obviously expect, until lunchtime to do so, for we are meeting friend Lestrade at the mortuary at half-past ten. It is already ten, and although fortunately the one involved is but a few minutes' walk from Baker Street, I would like it to be said that I did not rush you off your feet.'

I changed into my morning suit, as befitted a medical practitioner, but noted that Holmes simply donned his elderly green pea-jacket and a tweed cap. I chose a dark greatcoat, buttoning it high against the cold, and we started the short walk to one of those warehouse-type repositories which the police use to store cadavers. This one, at the far end of George Street, proved to be extremely dingy on the outside and not much brighter within. The bodies lay upon their slabs, draped with cloths making them take on perhaps a more sinister appearance than had they been undraped.

On the stroke of half-past ten Lestrade entered and joined us at the side of the latest addition to this group of poor wretched corpses fast becoming notorious as the Long Acre Victims. He nodded crustily to us both. 'Morning, Mr Holmes, Doctor; glad you could join me. I think I have a case here that will be just up your street. I wondered if my wire would bring you here, and I'm glad it did. Of course all this vampire business seems at first to be a lot of nonsense but the fact remains that we appear to have three murder victims, bitten on the throat and their blood sucked! Rum do, isn't it?'

Holmes smiled ironically and said, 'If your description of the cause and circumstances of death is accurate, Lestrade, it would be more than rum. Has one of your own medical men opined it to be so?'

Lestrade shrugged and said, 'Why

not ask him for yourself? He can tell you more than I can. I'll send for him, for he is here in this building.'

The inspector signalled to a medical assistant who had been hovering in the background and bade him fetch Dr Jarvis, who duly made an entrance: a stout man in surgeon's white coat. Lestrade introduced us and Holmes asked him, 'Dr Jarvis, I would be obliged if you would tell me what you consider to be the cause of Miss Joseph's demise?'

Dr Jarvis pulled back the cloth which covered this latest victim to reveal the head, neck and shoulders. There appeared the face of a young woman with a deathly pallor which seemed in advance of that which one would expect even on a cadaver. The pallor was so extreme that the newspaper reports of this victim having been deprived of so much blood seemed reasonable. I noticed the two symmetrical wounds on the throat, which did indeed suggest the victim of a vampire; yet would only do

37

so if one had read Stoker's novel or seen Irving's play. Holmes gazed at the tragic face and throat with deep interest. Then he asked, 'Do you, for instance, consider that her blood was drained by some living creature?'

Jarvis seemed surprised at the question. 'You see for yourself, do you not, the wounds near the jugular and the unearthly pallor? It is obvious, is it not?'

'You mean you have looked for no other injury or cause for her demise?'

'What more could there be: to have her blood drained would be enough to cause death, surely?'

He was slightly ironic in his tone as if dealing with laymen, which in Holmes's case of course he was. But as medical man I understood what was in Holmes's mind. So I said, 'Would it not be possible that the killer was trying to give the impression of a bizarre murder with a method inspired by Bram Stoker?'

Jarvis became somewhat defensive. 'Of course, it is Dr Watson, is it not?

Well, Doctor, why do you not give us the general practitioner's opinion.'

I knew that I was not expert in his job, yet neither, I suspected, was he but I took him at his word, removing my cuff links and turning back my shirt sleeves and those of my coat. I called for some cleansing agent and was given some surgical spirit. Using this and a pad of cotton waste I rubbed gently at the cheek of the dead girl. The deathly pallor gave way first to a cosmetic mask and finally to a complexion normal enough in death.

I said, 'The unnatural pallor is caused by the application of some form of powder, over this thick cosmetic base.'

Jarvis started and said, defensively, 'One could only assume the draining of blood, when the pallor was allied to those wounds which appear to have been caused by fangs.'

Holmes had been watching and listening with an encouraging air to my words and actions. He said, 'The wounds are not of a kind which one might have expected to cause instant death. Indeed, they do not appear to have resulted in the loss of a great deal of blood.'

Dr Jarvis snapped, 'Exactly! They have been sucked clean . . . '

But he spoke now without conviction. Holmes continued, 'So you have not looked much further for a cause of death than an assumption based upon a deathly pallor and two quite small throat wounds? Well, Watson, it may not be your field, but what would you have looked for if it were?'

I said, 'Some other wound or injury of a more serious nature. I am assuming, though, that some kind of general examination took place?'

Jarvis glared at me and said, 'Take my word that there are no other wounds upon the body.'

Lestrade broke in, 'We must defer to Dr Jarvis's assurance upon that. Well, Holmes, Dr Watson, what else would you have looked for?'

My friend looked at me and I read from his expression that he knew what I would say and wished me to say it. I said, 'I would be inclined to look for a broken neck.'

Jarvis said, 'Nonsense, there is no reason to suspect that.'

Lestrade, as diplomatic as was possible, said, 'Dr Jarvis, would you be kind enough to be sure that no such injury has occurred?'

'If you insist upon it, Inspector, but surely you must realize that such an injury would have been obvious to me.'

I intervened, 'Only if the body were moved from its present position upon the slab.'

'There was no reason to do so', Jarvis snapped, 'with such obvious cause of death but I will examine the neck if you wish, though it will be a waste of time.'

He started to lift the body by the shoulders and at once we could see that our suspicions concerning the neck injury were correct from the way in which the head dropped back. Jarvis examined the neck and then allowed me to confirm that the neck had indeed been broken.

I nodded to Holmes who then commented, 'An easy enough method of dispatch for a man of considerable strength. So the wound and powdering of the complexion were carried out to give the impression of a vampire-type of murder. Therefore we are looking for a killer who is looking for notoriety and cashing in upon the public interest in Stoker's *Dracula*. I believe that you will find that it is a similar story with the other two victims. Further examination will reveal broken necks and powdered faces.'

He took the envelope into which he had stored the powder that we had found, then continued, 'Inspector, if you take samples from the faces of the three victims and compare this trace of powder found in Long Acre, it will confirm my belief. I have no doubt that Dr Jarvis has a microscope upon these premises that you can use. Indeed, I feel sure that he could be prevailed upon to perform the experiment. He is, after all, the most qualified among us to do so.'

There was no trace of irony in Holmes's voice, for he was trying to seek the co-operation of the surgeon. At the same time Jarvis was trying to regain face and so was extremely willing to help. He confirmed that Holmes was right in assuming that all three victims had been made up to appear drained of blood by the use of the same substance. Then he and I made a more careful examination of the throat wounds and found them, in each case, to be scarcely deep enough to draw more than a trace of blood.

We repaired, Lestrade, Holmes and myself, to a hostelry which was adjacent to the premises and were at last able to discuss the matter freely.

Lestrade was the first to touch upon the subject which he found an embarrassment. 'You realize, Mr Holmes, that I have no direct control over the medical staff. I have always suspected Jarvis's credentials, but it is not up to me.'

Holmes replied, 'Pray do not concern yourself, Lestrade: a surgeon who does not dare to question being addressed as Doctor had led me to suspect them myself. But I have no doubt that it is a grisly job, not one that a highly qualified man would fight to gain. Watson may be a humble general practitioner but would serve far better than Jarvis at the post.'

I knew not if I should take Holmes's remarks as a compliment or a patronizing comment, so I decided to ignore his words. But Lestrade took them up. 'Well, Dr Watson, if you are looking for a post I could put in a good word for you!'

Lestrade's words demanded my answer. 'Inspector, whilst thanking you for your kindness, I must tell you that I am fully occupied with my practice most of the time. But my employment is of little interest. May I ask you what you have made of the wounds on the throat of each victim. They would appear to be made by the same implement.'

The inspector's reply was a trifle vague. 'Oh, some sort of fork perhaps? The space between the wounds is the same in each case. Yes, some sort of fork, that is assuming that we completely rule out the Dracula idea?'

Holmes had said little but made up for it next. 'Rule out? I have never ruled *in* such a theory! When I read Stoker's *Dracula* I took it to be exactly what it is: a bizarre novel showing great imagination. The only vampire that exists is a small bat which lives by taking blood from cattle.'

I interjected, 'How do you account for the fact that the cattle are unharmed and yet human victims become fatally ill?'

'I do not account for it, Watson. The few human beings to be bitten by these bats have survived. Just a tiny number have displayed symptoms of hydrophobia, with which they could as easily have been infected by a rabid dog, cat or rabbit. You have been taking Stoker's book too seriously; come, you are a scientist, pray be scientific in your view of this matter.'

I was lost for words concerning the legendary bats so I returned to reality. 'What, then, of this fork that Lestrade suggests as the probable cause of the wounds?'

He considered. 'I believe it could have been a tuning fork. I have a good eye for measurement, and I believe the space between the prongs is such that the effect which we have seen might make that instrument the likely one. If Lestrade has been thinking in terms of a fork used in a trade, my diagnosis might be useful.'

The inspector was a little dubious. 'A butcher would, to my mind, be more likely to commit such a crime than would, shall we say, a violin teacher.'

Holmes shrugged. 'There could be something in what you say, my dear Lestrade, and there are hundreds of trade instruments that would bear measurement. But perhaps more important is the proximity of Long Acre to the Lyceum, and the very subject of Irving's play. Not coincidental surely. You could be looking for someone who wishes Irving harm.'

Then Lestrade said something that amazed both Holmes and me. 'So you reckon that we should rule Irving himself right out?'

I started, then said, 'Surely Irving's an unlikely enough candidate for a murderer, and can account for his time where it is necessary?'

Lestrade said, 'The actual murder probably occurred at a time when Irving was assumed to be taking a nap, having already dressed and made himself up prior to his call. Evidently this is his habit.'

I countered, 'The stage door-keeper might be able to tell you if he left the theatre; he would have to have returned before his call too, in full dress and make-up.'

The inspector considered and then said, 'He could have left and returned by means of his dressing room window. The alley outside is usually deserted and his dresser takes a break at about that time.'

But Holmes was very definite when he said, 'The three murders were not committed in a pattern that would allow this: moreover, examination of the window will tell you that it would be impossible for Irving to have left and entered by that means.'

Lestrade nodded knowingly. 'Too small, I suppose?'

Holmes nodded. 'Too small, Lestrade; I would have trouble getting in or out of the building by that means myself and I am something of a contortionist, as you know. Irving is a broadly built man who would have found it quite impossible.'

We were not, Holmes and I, regular patrons of this particular hostelry or known to its landlord or customers yet it was soon obvious to me that Lestrade was, for the establishment which had been reasonably busy when we entered soon thinned out as far as other patrons were concerned. I remarked upon this to the inspector who grinned as he said, 'I have an arrangement with Ernie, the guv'nor. He gives me a certain amount of information (after all, he hears a great deal concerning wrongdoing past, present and future); in return I do not stay here for very long at a time. In fact, I do believe I have outstayed my welcome!'

He referred to the fact that the landlord was making his way to the alcove in which we sat. 'Everything all right, Inspector?'

Lestrade replied, 'Well enough, Ernie, though I would be interested in anything you might have learned concerning these Long Acre crimes.'

'The vampire, old Dracula? I'm hardly likely to hear much about that, sir. As you know, my clientele are, some of them, now and again involved in petty crime. We gets burglars, dips, street corner bookies, that sort of thing.

But I don't remember you ever nabbing a murderer through anything that I was able to tell you. Still, if you was just asking my opinion on it I'd say it was a very strange affair indeed. If I were you I would be watching Sir Henry Irving like a hawk and of course I would be interested in any visiting Hungarians that happened to be around.'

The inspector said, 'I get your point about the Hungarians, Ernie, but I fail to find any reason to suspect Sir Henry Irving.'

Ernie replied, 'You know some of these actors will do anything for publicity. There was an actor who used to come in here at one time who was appearing in a play about Jack the Ripper. We get a lot of ladies in here who are no better than they should be. He used to ogle them and draw his finger across his throat. Terrified of him they were.'

Lestrade chuckled. 'But surely, Ernie, you do not think that he *was* the Ripper?'

The publican considered. 'Well . . . you know they never caught him, did they?'

I noticed that Sherlock Holmes kept very quiet, obviously wishing to preserve his anonymity. We made to leave the premises to the marked relief of the landlord.

The inspector said, 'I will be seeing you, Ernie . . . '

'Right you are, Inspector, but . . . not too soon, eh?'

We bade farewell to Lestrade, Holmes having at least aided his investigations to some extent. No longer did he need to search for some bloodsucking Dracula in human form but rather to a flesh-and-blood killer who wished him to gain that impression.

'Why, Watson, why does he do it?'

We were taking afternoon tea at 221B as Holmes pondered the question. He had reached down Stoker's novel and numerous files from the shelf and had these spread around him. Tiring of his buttered muffin he searched for the right pipe to suit his mood, then after consideration decided upon the old favourite clay: its mouthpiece so worn that I wondered if it had once been a churchwarden. Charging it with Scottish mixture from the Turkish slipper, he enquired, 'Watson, do you have a box of vestas? I have mislaid mine.'

I wondered how a mind that had shown such brilliance in finding countless missing persons and artefacts could possibly lose a box of vestas but said nothing as I handed him my own. He struck one and lit his pipe and tossed my box on to the table, saying (as if reading my mind), 'I could find them, Watson, should I wish to waste my thoughts upon trivialities. I prefer to dwell upon the Vampire of Long Acre. Assuming, as we both do, that Sir Henry is entirely blameless in this series of bizarre events, why on earth would anyone commit a series of horrific crimes and risk apprehension by drawing attention to himself?'

'You mean in assuming the Dracula disguise?'

'Certainly, and why does he choose Long Acre, where the chances of detection must surely increase with each barbaric slaying. It can only be because he wishes to harm Irving that he takes such great risks.'

'Holmes, I realize of course that Sir Henry is incapable, either physically or through intent, of such deeds. Is there not yet some possibility in what Ernie the landlord of that public house opined?'

'You mean his inference that actors will do anything to gain notoriety? Well, I take your point; you mean that even though Irving is so clearly innocent, could not some manager or person involved with the finances of the play be capable of such horrendous advertising methods?'

I was horrified at his spoken version of what had indeed been in my mind. One thing to think such thoughts, but to hear their recitation aloud is quite another.

'You surely do not harbour even the minute thought that Irving might be party to such a scoundrel's plan?'

'I have to consider every possibility, Watson, but I do not think it likely that Sir Henry is implicated in any way. Moreover, at the present time the effect upon business at the Lyceum is detrimental. Any manager or financier would surely be astute enough to anticipate that in this instance the publicity would cause more harm than good.'

My reply was interrupted by Mrs Hudson with news of a caller. 'Sir Henry Irving to see Mr Holmes.'

Holmes was a little surprised at an event which for once he had not predicted. He indicated that the actor should be admitted and the eminent thespian entered, resplendent in dark cloak and broad-brimmed hat. 'Forgive me, Holmes, for giving no warning of my arrival. I was in the vicinity and decided to chance it.'

As I pulled back the best armchair,

Holmes put him at his ease. 'You have caught me at a moment of inactivity, Sir Henry. We are taking tea, yet your problems are not far from my mind. You will observe that I am surrounded by ephemera concerning the Transylvanian fiend!'

Sir Henry smiled politely and said, 'Yes, well, I came to tell you that I plan to close my season at the Lyceum. I can see no other way, having cast an eye upon the advance booking plan.'

He spoke the words with a studied shake and timbre as though they had been spoken by the ghost of Hamlet's father. His eyes rolled in the true tradition of theatrical tragedy. He added, rather more matter-of-factly, 'I shall shelve *Dracula* until all this ghastly business is done. I can always revive one of my old successes and then I feel sure that the public will quickly forget.'

Holmes was contemplative as he said, 'Had it occurred to you to transfer the play to another area, another town perhaps? For example, if you were to present the play in Birmingham and there were no tragedies of the Long Acre kind in that city you would have laid the ghost of any sort of connection.'

'But what if the tragic happenings were to continue in the region of Long Acre?'

Holmes considered. 'That would be unfortunate, but clearly such events could not be married with yourself further.'

'By George, Holmes, you are right! I could present the play for a season at the Theatre Royal, Brighton, which I happen to know is dark at present. It is a beautiful old theatre, and its period quality would lend itself to the production. I say, your advice has been well worth the price of admission, what?'

He departed, to give that which proved to be the final performance of *Dracula* at the Lyceum, at least for quite some time.

After he had left I unburdened myself to Holmes concerning certain aspects of the matter. 'So does this mean that you will go to Brighton to observe matters and leave the Long Acre murders in the sole hands of Inspector Lestrade?'

His answer surprised me. 'On the contrary, Watson, I will be giving Lestrade all the help I can; no matter if he wants it or not. You, however, will be off to the queen of watering places to watch over Irving!'

I started, though quickly recovering my composure. 'You know that I will be of whatever assistance I can to you, Holmes. The season for Brighton is not ideal, but I shall go stoutly shod and well wrapped.'

3

Transylvania By The Sea

As soon as we had heard the definite details of Irving's retreat to Brighton, I made my own plans to follow him. I decided that I would put up at a small hotel with which I was familiar, in Oriental Place, a steeply hilled square of Regency origin which faced the seafront. I planned to send daily written reports to Baker Street, on the understanding that I would wire if anything really drastic should occur.

'I shall await your reports with the greatest of interest and reliance, Watson. You have always been a first-class aide, and I have as ever the greatest of confidence in you.'

Holmes's words could only add to my determination to play my own small part in the apprehension of the fiend who murdered persons, seemingly in a quite indiscriminate manner. Of course I realized that I was almost certainly going to Brighton upon a wild-goose chase for I could not believe that this maniac (for what else could he be?) was about to move his scene of terror in the mistaken idea of incriminating someone as august as Sir Henry Irving.

So it was then that within a week I found myself occupying a front-row stall of the beautiful old theatre in Brighton. Doubtless had it been summertime with the consequent invasion of the visitors and holidaymakers I would have sat with several hundred fellow patrons. As it was there were enough people in the audience to discount any feeling of failure, yet not quite enough to indicate a resounding success at the box office. Irving was well received and so was the play; yet even here, more than fifty miles from the scene of the Dracula murders, one could sense a certain reserve, or uneasiness. All of this and anything else

I could observe that might be considered to be even faintly useful was conveyed by me to Holmes by the very first morning post. There was little to report, however, there being no news of gruesome deeds either in Brighton or near Long Acre.

I decided not to enter the stage door after the performance, feeling that the less immediate contact between Sir Henry and myself for a while the better. But I kept my eyes and ears open, noticing that Sir Henry had brought his own small orchestra with him to grace the pit with their presence. Then, whilst on musical matters, I was able to tell Holmes about the itinerant violinist who played outside the stage door of the Theatre Royal. I had been told by the stage manager that he had been a fixture there for many years; tall, thin, stooped and grey-bearded. I dropped a sixpence into his shabby violin case as I passed. He grunted his thanks and I took a slow stroll along the Kings Road, down West Street and along the sea front in the direction of Oriental Place. I turned my collar against the wind which was not merely chilly but drove sea spray onto the promenade at regular intervals.

On my second day in Brighton with there having been no news of tragedies of the kind which concerned us (either in London or Brighton), I began to feel rather useless, like being on a holiday that one neither desired nor enjoyed. A completely unproductive day was broken only by meals and a meeting with Sir Henry in his dressing room.

He greeted me with optimism in his rich, mellow voice. 'Ah, Watson, my dear fellow, pray be seated whilst Jennings finishes helping me to disguise myself as Count Dracula. I trust you have found some good diggings, what?'

Inwardly I chuckled at the thought of the neat little hotel in Oriental Place being referred to as 'diggings' whilst outwardly I replied, 'Comfortable enough, sir, and I am relieved that you have not as yet been tortured by events like those which plagued you in the vicinity of the Lyceum.'

He lifted his hands in a truly theatrical gesture of mock horror. 'Speak not too soon lest the fates hear thee and mar thy joy with a resurgence of woe!'

I was impressed. 'Shakespeare?'

'No, Henry Irving. I made it up on the spur of the moment, Watson, but it's not bad, eh?'

I chuckled obediently, then said, 'I take your point, sir, that we must count no poultry. Let us indeed pray for no recurrence and that the murderer will soon be apprehended, even should his butchery cease forthwith.'

Sir Henry agreed and then invited me to use the Royal Box. 'It is scarcely used now, but by tradition it is kept for the use of the Queen. It is only used today when a celebrity arrives without having had the sense to reserve a seat and the house is full.'

Even the most comfortable of orchestra stalls could scarce rival the luxury of an armchair in a Royal Box, and I was pleased to lean forward over the padded red velvet and perceive a healthy house present to see the play. After the performance I thanked my benefactor who implied that the box would be made permanently available to me during my stay in Brighton.

The reader may have had his nerves lulled into a sense of false security by my past few paragraphs, yet I fear that my own feeling of crisis past was about to explode in fearful shock. For on the night which followed, I had dropped into the theatre, more through boredom than anything else, deciding to watch the third act, yet again, from my Royal Box.

Seated comfortably I was rudely interrupted by a news-seller intruding through the velvet entrance drape. He thrust a broadsheet right under my nose. ''Orrible murder in London . . . the Long Acre Vampire strikes again!'

I thrust a copper coin at him and

started to digest the front-page headline feature of Brighton's *Evening Argus*. It gave an account of yet another dreadful killing which bore all of those only too familiar trademarks:

THE 'VAMPIRE' OF LONG ACRE

At roughly half-past seven of this evening another bizarre slaying occurred in close vicinity to London's Long Acre. This time the victim was an elderly man, evidently a visitor from Tunbridge Wells as far as it has been possible to discover from an examination of the contents of his pockets. He had the pallid look and wounds upon the throat of the previous victims as if attacked by a fanged animal, yet the actual cause of death was a broken neck.

That brilliant Scotland Yard detective, Inspector Lestrade, revealed his discovery that the wounds were merely superficial, administered to give the impression that the victim's life-blood had been drained, this impression enhanced by the application of cosmetic powder to give a pallid appearance. As with the previous killings in the area a strange cloaked figure was observed retreating from the scene.

When asked by our reporter how he had discovered the actual cause of death and the false nature of the vampire factor, he said, 'After so many years in this job one gets a sort of sixth sense. With traces of powder around and the superficial nature of the throat wound one naturally looked for another cause of death. Call it intuition if you like.'

I had very mixed feelings from reading this account. Feelings of horror that this ghastly killer had struck again, relief that it had occurred, however, in London when Sir Henry was safely far enough from the crime scene to have his obvious innocence enhanced. But this feeling of relief was dashed to the ground at the raising of the curtain.

When Count Dracula appeared I had only to glance at him to realize that it was not Sir Henry Irving! I watched the rest of the performance in something of a trance. Then with the final curtains taken I rushed to Sir Henry's dressing room. There I found Jennings performing his nightly final job of putting Dracula to rest, taking a wig of longish grey hair from the head of an actor other than Sir Henry. When I enquired as to the reason for the substitution I was told that Sir Henry was off. Jennings explained, 'Officially, Doctor, the understudy is only supposed to appear in the event of illness or injury. But what actually happens is that the principal, like Sir Henry, allows the understudy a certain very small number of appearances during the run. This is Joe Barton and tonight was his first crack of the whip since we opened at the Lyceum. In fact, Sir Henry was tired and decided to stay in London just to give Joe a stab at the part. That aside he had some business to transact at the Lyceum.'

I all but staggered back to my hotel, unable to fully comprehend how fate could be so cruel, aye, or Irving to be so lax in not even informing Holmes or myself regarding his plans.

I wired Holmes to the effect that I would return to confer with him and I did indeed take the early-morning train to Victoria. Then, when I reached 221B, I almost wished that I had stayed in Brighton.

Holmes was in a furious mood. 'Upon my word, Watson, must I do everything myself? You should not have let Sir Henry Irving out of your sight, let alone allow him to return to London completely without your knowledge, or mine. What on earth possessed him to do it after the whole Brighton enterprise had been arranged to prevent such an occurrence?'

I made things worse for myself by

showing Holmes the front page of the *Brighton Argus*, and Lestrade made things bad for himself by calling to see Holmes!

'Upon my word, Inspector, I am amazed that you have the time to call upon me. Why are you not at Scotland Yard exercising that sixth sense which you have acquired after so many years as a 'brilliant detective'?'

To add insult to injury, Lestrade had not seen that particular paper and he scanned it with growing embarrassment. 'I never said it like that, Mr Holmes, I was misquoted. In fact, I was going to explain that you had been of some slight help to me when the reporter fellow suddenly wasn't there.'

Holmes grunted. 'Well, never mind all that, let us hasten to speak with Sir Henry. You can join us, Lestrade. Do you have a police vehicle with you?'

Lestrade studied his boots as he replied, 'Yes, I will take you to see him.'

The inspector spoke very quietly to the driver of the four-wheeled growler, and after a few minutes Holmes remarked, 'Lestrade, your driver has taken the wrong turning. Sir Henry resides in north London!'

The policeman was very sheepish as he explained, 'We are on our way to the central police station where they are holding Sir Henry pending further enquiries.'

Holmes all but exploded. 'You have arrested Sir Henry Irving?'

'Yes, I had to, Holmes, it was more than my job was worth to leave him at liberty. He comes back from Brighton, all but secretly, and another murder occurs with him having just left the Lyceum where he was talking with the manager.'

'Until what time?'

'Until about seven. He was unable to establish a presence anywhere between seven and half-past the hour.'

'Do you suspect him yourself, Lestrade?'

'No, but all the suspicions will point to him. But do not worry, I can release him into your care if you will take the responsibility. He may later be officially charged with the crime, unless we can find the real criminal meanwhile!'

Holmes became remarkably calm and said very little until we reached the police station. Lestrade led the way to a cell where Sir Henry was being held. The noble thespian presented a woeful presence that quite equalled anything I feel sure that he had enacted upon the stage. He sat at a rough wooden table in a hard-backed chair; the only other cell furnishings being a cot of the usual kind and a washstand with bowl and water jug. Although his luxuriant hair had been tended, his collar was missing and he was unshaven. He rose as we entered with an expression that held a gleam of hope amid his obvious despair.

He spoke, and although his voice had lost none of its timbre it was filled with anguish and desperation. 'Holmes, Watson, see what I have finally come to! A long and noble career has finally brought me to plunge downward, into a common prison cell. I played a half-mad convict in *The Wanderer* and the part gave me one of the high points of my career, but this is real. I have been forced to sleep upon a hard straw mattress. Oh, what would Lady Irving think if she could see me now? I was allowed to send a message to her to the effect that I had decided to sleep at my club. I have no doubt that the committee will shortly meet to expel me from that august fraternity. Alas, what am I to do? You must help me, Holmes, you must help me!'

It had been an amazing speech which neither Holmes nor I had dared to interrupt, nor had Lestrade or the gaoler. It was my firm belief that much as he resented his situation, he somehow revelled in the opportunity to speak lines that he uttered. I resisted the familiarity of laying a hand upon his shoulder and left it to my friend to console him. This he did, but not without some criticism. 'My dear Sir

Henry, I sympathize with the situation which you find yourself in, of course, but it would have been entirely avoided had you stayed on at Brighton or at the very least informed either Watson or myself regarding your movements. I am tempted to leave you here just to teach you a lesson. However, this would not be a politic thing. If you stay here longer the newspapers will get wind of it. I can pull strings to keep your arrest a secret and you can be released into my care. This is a responsibility that I am inclined to accept if you will be guided by my suggestions.'

Sir Henry wrung his hands and pleaded, 'I will accept any advice that you are good enough to give, in return for being released from this ignominy and degradation!'

Holmes took full responsibility for Sir Henry Irving, signing documents that promised that he would produce our client if and when required. No publicity having so far been attracted we could be fairly safe in leaving the police station with the noble thespian and transporting him to his home. This we did, and my friend refrained from discussing the matter in hand whilst we were still in the cab. Once we were safely within the portals of Irving Towers (as the actor's imposing residence was titled), it was a different matter.

As Lady Irving dispensed coffee, Holmes gave his instructions. 'You are to stay within the precincts of your home, Sir Henry, without as much as showing your face at a window. To all intents and purposes you will be appearing as usual at Brighton. Only Lestrade will be informed of your real address and a plain-clothes officer will stay here with you so that your presence here can be vouched for at all times. Meanwhile, an understudy will play Dracula, but not the actor who played the part last evening.'

I broke in with a word at this point. 'Holmes, if an understudy continues in the role, no matter who he might be, the public at large will know that Sir Henry is not in Brighton, which if I have gained the meaning of your words is not the impression you are hoping to make.'

Holmes explained, 'Whilst safely here, under secret house arrest, Sir Henry will be impersonated in Brighton by an understudy, both on and off the stage. This imposter will, with your help, play the part of Sir Henry Irving as well as that of Dracula. I say with your help, Watson, because I intend to send you back to Brighton in the role of dresser. Friend Jennings will be given a paid holiday, for no impersonation could succeed at such close quarters. It will be your task to do all in your power, Watson, to aid this imperson-ation, keeping everyone else as far from Sir Henry as is possible.'

I gasped at the daring of this plan. 'But Holmes, where are you going to find an understudy who can fill these requirements? Moreover, how can you be sure that he will preserve the secrecy that his task will demand?'

Sherlock Holmes smiled a mocking smile. 'I intend to play the dual roles of Sir Henry Irving and Count Dracula myself. Come, Watson, you have often said that the stage was robbed of a first-class actor when I took up my profession.'

I muttered in bewildered fashion, leaving it to Sir Henry to point out the difficulties in Holmes's daring plan. 'My dear Holmes, whilst I appreciate all that you are doing for me, I fail to see how you can disguise yourself thoroughly enough as this poor play actor, let alone learn the part of Dracula in time.'

Holmes nodded wisely, 'For that reason I will not replace your regular understudy until tomorrow night. I have what is known in this scientific age as a photographic memory, Sir Henry. I have the ability to study a page of text and commit it to recall. I have seen your performance and I have until well into tomorrow to study with you and perfect a disguise.'

Irving had at his home a perfect replica of a theatre dressing room, complete with his name upon the door. He took Holmes therein and I left them sitting there whilst Holmes studied the book of the play whilst Irving reminded him of the movements which would be involved. I spent three hours chatting with Lady Irving in the drawing room.

'Dr Watson, I do not fully understand this terrible business which Henry has become embroiled in, but I thank the heavens that he has two such kind and brilliant persons as yourself and Sherlock Holmes to aid him.'

I reassured her that we would do all we could. Then I tried to explain as best I could the exact nature of Sir Henry's predicament. I told her the whole story which she quickly understood, being quite obviously an extremely intelligent woman. I have found that so often the wife of a great man is treated rather as a child. Lady Irving deserved better treatment and I felt that the more she understood, the more she might be able to extend help to us. I ventured at length to ask her if she felt that Sir Henry had made any enemies of an unstable nature during his long career. She responded in quite a useful way. 'All actors are in my opinion unstable, Dr Watson; even Henry is himself eccentric! But as for enemies, he has I believe made less than most who have gained a position of fame.'

She was kind enough to show me albums of cast photographs from Irving's past productions. Her deft fingers pointed out this person and that with comments which were thorough enough to be counted as biographies in miniature. I could appreciate how valuable her comments could be and tried to commit to memory and notebook as much information as might be of value of Holmes. But alas, I had not his ability to photograph pages in my mind!

We were interrupted at about three in the afternoon by the entrance into the room of Sir Henry. He said, 'Irene, I appreciate that you have left Holmes and me to confer but should you not perhaps produce some sort of luncheon?'

She smiled at him. 'Henry, I had not forgotten. I have had the girl produce cold meat and salad against the doubt as to when you would be ready for it.'

She rose to make for the kitchen region, then suddenly stopping in her tracks, she gasped and pointed accusingly. 'You are not Henry! What can this mean?'

To my own amazement as well as hers, Sir Henry replied with the voice of Sherlock Holmes. 'Pray calm yourself, dear Lady Irving. It is I, Sherlock Holmes. I have taken the liberty of trying my great impersonation out upon you. To be honest I am amazed to have got away with it, even for the few seconds that I did!'

The lady quickly pulled herself together and said, 'Upon my word, Mr Holmes, it is like a miracle. You would deceive anyone. I only knew as I came nearer to you from the backs of your hands, or the left hand to be more exact. You see, Henry has a scar on the back of his left hand of a kind which would be difficult to disguise. He was injured by a falling piece of scenery at a theatre in Nottingham, many years ago, but the scar is still vivid.'

Holmes turned to me. 'You see, Watson, I am getting lax in some directions. I believe that the wearing of gloves at all times will take care of that problem.'

I still could not believe it; the luxuriant grey hair hung from Holmes's scalp to his collar in the exact style of Irving's. The gold pince-nez clipped onto the considerable nose which was as prominent as Holmes's but wider at the bridge. The complexion was exactly duplicated as was the stance and grey tweed suit. Most important of all, the voice had been a perfect imitation of the actor's voice. Then Sir Henry himself entered the room and the two of them stood side by side, for all the world like identical twins. I could not imagine how it had been managed.

Holmes explained the finer points of the miracle. 'I am afraid that I have to reveal one of Sir Henry's closely guarded secrets. He wears a collar-length wig and I am wearing his spare head of hair. The same goes for the pince-nez, and I have borrowed one of Sir Henry's suits of clothes. The facial make-up was simplicity itself and will be simple to maintain. Some powder, grey bushy eyebrows and a little paste at the bridge of the nose. The rest is just a matter of stance and vocal imitation. Fortunately we are of similar height. By the way, Sir Henry, I must ask for the loan of a pair of your white dress gloves.'

We do not, of course, always see ourselves as others see us, and it had taken a close shoulder-to-shoulder inspection in the dressing room mirror to convince Irving that Holmes's impersonation was brilliant.

Again the two of them went into close confine so that Holmes could make the most of what little coaching the great actor could give him in the time at their disposal. I was no longer in doubt that Holmes could pass as Irving except in the most intimate circumstances, yet I had concern regarding his ability to carry off the thespian aspect of his impersonation. Yes, it was true that I had often said and genuinely thought that Holmes could have made a great actor. But his ability to hold up a star role with practically no rehearsal — and bearing in mind Irving's great reputation — that was another matter. However, I could only hope that he would not need to try for more than two or three performances which might soon be forgotten and not affect Irving's reputation too much.

I was left again in the company of Lady Irving who urged that I sample the makeshift meal that had been prepared. She insisted that we take our meal in the dining room despite the almost alfresco atmosphere. She said, 'Everything is on the table, Doctor, and you will need to help yourself. I have sent the girl to her aunt's for a couple of days. I fear that she might remark to the milkman upon the subject should she be confronted with two Henrys!'

A practical thought struck me. 'How shall you explain the presence of Sir Henry when she returns, for she must know about the Brighton season?'

'I shall tell her that he is unwell and that the understudy is appearing for him. I do not believe she, or others that he might come upon, will be too curious.'

The dining room was splendid, though not large. Obviously the Irvings did not entertain upon a very large scale. Indeed the house itself was rather small, smaller that is than one would expect for the residence of our foremost actor.

I did not, of course, remark to that effect but coincidentally Lady Irving herself volunteered information upon that subject. 'As you have commented, Dr Watson, it is a very fine house, but it is a little small you know. But we have not been considering a transfer to larger premises because we are so comfortable here. Take the case of Henry's mementoes, posters, framed portraits and statuettes. They fill this room completely, yet would need to be spread thinly in a mansion.'

I glanced around the room and took her point completely. The framed items thoroughly filled two of the walls, arranged like a jigsaw puzzle without spaces between. Then at the end of the room there was a bay window with a large shelf, bearing the statuettes and busts of Sir Henry in his various roles. The curtains, which were drawn back so that these items could be seen, were of rich plum velvet, rather like theatre-house curtains, and the pelmet and side pieces were in the form of a proscenium arch, with comedy and tragedy masks at the top centre.

The perfect hostess, Lady Irene

pointed out the various framed items of interest, just as she had those in the drawing room. I found this all to be interesting and indeed would have done even had Holmes and I no connection with Irving, for he was a favourite actor of mine. There were the inevitable cast group photographs going back over fifty years with the earliest of them being somewhat stiff and formal when compared to the most recent examples. It was interesting to notice how faithful Irving was to many of his supporting players with many of the same faces appearing around him again and again over the years. I remarked for instance that Charles Mornington who played Van Helsing in the current production was also featured in many of the earlier groups. Indeed there was one framed example, dated some twenty years earlier, where Irving and Mornington stood centre stage in identical costume and make-up.

Lady Irene explained, 'Henry and Charles shared the top billing for

The Corsican Brothers but thereafter Charles never gained that status again. However, Henry has always considered him for any suitable role in his productions and I think Mornington has done quite well in the profession. A very nice man by the way, and never any sign of resentment from him. Not like Ashley Barrington, for example. He got the role of Renfrew, quite an important casting, but he appears to believe that he should have played the lead. He has always shown signs of envy yet Henry has used him frequently in his productions.' She dropped her voice. 'Only goes to show what a thoroughly decent husband I have got.'

I murmured in assent and felt that I had already learned facts that would be of interest to Sherlock Holmes, though I did not see him again for several hours.

When Holmes and Irving reappeared they were each in their own persona, for Holmes had removed the make-up and clothes that had made him into Irving's double. The actor and the detective devoured some of the cold meal that had been left for them and Lady Irene and I sat at the table, at least able to keep them company with a glass of wine.

The great actor was full of praise for his pupil. 'I must say, Holmes is getting on splendidly as Count Dracula! He is a natural actor, you know: you would swear that he was a professional.'

Holmes smiled politely and said, 'Sir Henry flatters me. My art is that of an impersonator. I can duplicate a character, but must of course have a great example to follow. Had I been asked to play Count Dracula from scratch without Sir Henry's example, I would I fear flounder. But I think I can safely say that we will get away with it, at least for a couple of performances. But remember, I have the days to get through. I believe I will feign minor illness, with my personal physician, Dr John Watson, to protect me from too close a contact with anyone. Long walks, suitably muffled, and long periods closeted with my doctor will be the order of the day.'

Lady Irene smiled gratefully and said, 'My dear Mr Holmes, I cannot thank you enough for the effort you have put into helping Henry with this terrible business. Were it not for you he would at this moment be languishing in a prison cell. In comparison, the irritation of being house-bound will be a minor one. I feel sure that one so resourceful will bring this business to a satisfactory close.'

Before we retired to the room that Lady Irene had prepared for us, Holmes was also treated to an exploration of the theatrical ephemera. Later in the Irving's spare bedroom we compared notes upon these nostalgic mementoes.

'Shall you give consideration to what Lady Irene said about Ashley Barrington?'

'Watson, I give consideration to everything of which I am aware. But I think the envy of one actor for another must not be taken too seriously. After all, there is also the matter of Charles Mornington, whose envy may be there but better disguised. But anyone with a long association with Irving certainly needs to be given consideration, as does the presence of non-actors who appear in some of the photographs.'

I confess that I had not noticed this particular phenomenon. 'In which photographs did members of the public appear?'

'Why, in several of those where the cast were posed in the open air; in some cases in front of the theatre façades. In some of these, persons unconnected with the play can be seen looking on with interest from the foreground. I did notice one or two faces that were to be seen in several of these pictures; they are, I imagine, admirers who turn up at any place where their favourite actor may be seen.'

Before attempting to sleep, Holmes studied again the typewritten sheets that included the lines that he would have to speak upon the morrow. His final word that night: 'You know, Watson, that which is studied immediately before slumber is the more easily remembered when required. Just a little trick that I learned back in my student days.'

4

The Lanes

The following morning we travelled to Brighton in Irving's splendid motor car. It was driven by a hired driver, Sir Henry having given his usual man a short holiday, at Holmes's suggestion. This meant that Holmes could travel in his Henry Irving disguise quite safely, even if I did have to address Holmes as 'Sir Henry' during conversation and be very careful what I said. However, I considered that this was excellent practice for what we would face upon our arrival at the Theatre Royal.

When we stopped for refreshment it was Holmes's very first chance to try his impersonation in public. Irving's profile and general appearance were far too well publicized to allow anything else. It was fortunate that the weather was chilly as this allowed Holmes to be well muffled with a scarf. He wound this around his neck so that only his prominent nose appeared. As his 'Doctor' I was able to explain to the waiter that he had an illness of the throat. That worthy evidently had served Irving at some time and made sure that we knew it. However, what he did say was reassuring to us. 'Ah, Sir Henry, what can I fetch you? An omelette is it, like last time?'

I explained, 'Sir Henry has a sore throat. We are worried for his voice. Yes please, fetch him an omelette.'

Holmes, carried away with his success, removed the scarf and smiled at the waiter when he brought our refreshments.

'That's better, Sir Henry, you look a little brighter already. You remember me, Howlett, don't you?'

Holmes, further emboldened spoke, like Sir Henry but in a husky tone, 'Of course, Howlett, please excuse my voice. Good to see you again.'

The waiter smiled. 'Watch that Hobson's now, sir. I believe gargling with port is good for a dodgy Hobson's.'

I assumed it was rhyming slang which I knew Holmes would understand.

As we made our way back to the motor car, Holmes was positively optimistic regarding his impersonation.

The arrival at the Theatre Royal of 'Sir Henry Irving' was beautifully stage-managed by Sherlock Holmes. As the car drew close to the stage door he daringly descended from it and instead of sneaking in past the stage doorkeeper he stood, head held high, and holding the post for several seconds as he had seen Sir Henry do. A reporter from the *Argus* suddenly made a mysterious appearance and my friend even ventured a short interview in his new guise, keeping his voice ever so slightly husky yet unmistakably that of the knight of the theatre.

'Sir Henry, you have been out of the

play and indisposed, we notice. Yet you seem well enough now.'

'I am well recovered save for a little trouble with my throat which shall not be allowed to keep me longer from my beloved public, what?'

'What do you make of the series of murders which have come to be called the work of 'The Vampire of Long Acre'? Is your playing the part of Count Dracula at the Lyceum, so close to Long Acre, a pure coincidence?'

'You refer no doubt to the retreating figure of 'Count Dracula' seen at the vicinity of each crime? I am alas too frail and elderly to flee down Long Acre, dear boy! But you can inform your readers that I am horrified, just as they must be, to hear of such terrible events.'

'Why do you not close down your play, in case there is more than coincidence?'

'If I thought it would make any difference I would do so. The murderer must be deranged and would doubtless continue his ghastly deeds and will, I imagine, do so until apprehended: possibly disguised as George Robey, near the Alhambra Music Hall?'

With the greatest respect to Sir Henry Irving, I felt that my friend had handled the situation beautifully and possibly more diplomatically than the actor himself would have done. Moreover, he had established that Irving was back at the Theatre Royal, which was one of our main aims.

Inside, Holmes did not linger to gossip with the various persons who were going about their business of preparing for the performance. Instead he hurried toward the dressing room that bore Irving's name and waved airily to all and sundry as he passed. Jennings was waiting in the doorway of the room and Holmes now faced the acid test of his disguise. I knew that he did not intend to try and deceive the dresser upon any lengthy basis, but I realized that he would like to see how long he could do so.

'Sir Henry! Welcome back. I do hope you are feeling better, in fact are completely recovered?'

'Thank you, Jennings, I am better, but still my throat troubles me, so I have brought Dr Watson, whom you have already met, to minister to my vocal problems.'

Jennings was, I realized by his reply, quite shrewd and quick upon the uptake. He looked keenly at Holmes. 'The throat trouble developed then whilst you were in London recovering from an extremely minor ailment, designed as I remember purely to give the deputy a fair crack of the whip?'

Holmes looked sharply at Jennings, saying, 'Quite so, if one feigns illness, that malady often descends upon one. But no matter, I am all but myself again and looking forward to this evening's performance.'

'Well, sir, all is ready, your costume is cleaned and hung, and your Dracula wig is on the block and I will start the make-up as usual when you are ready and rested. I assume you would like to take your usual siesta upon the couch before I begin?'

Holmes grunted his approval and Jennings took his jacket and hung it beside the greatcoat already on the rack. Then he hesitated, at length saying, 'I'll take your gloves, sir, shall I?'

It was Holmes's turn to hesitate, then he peeled off the gloves and handed them to Jennings. The dresser's face took on an enigmatic expression as he placed the gloves in a drawer. Then he turned back to face my friend, looking him full in the face and saying, 'I don't know quite what this game is that you are playing with me, Mr Sherlock Holmes!'

Holmes chuckled and then replied, 'All will be made clear to you, my dear Jennings. But first as a matter of interest how long did it take you to see through my disguise?'

'Two or three minutes, Mr Holmes, for it is a great impersonation. It has to be, does it not, to deceive an actor's dresser for even a very short time.'

'When did you first suspect something was amiss?'

'The moment before I suggested that you take a siesta. I cannot give the reason for my first doubt, but I decided to put it to the test. You see, Sir Henry usually takes a nap when all the work has been done on his make-up and never before. When you assented so instantly to this reversal of the habits of a quarter of a century I knew that there was something strange. Then I noticed that you had retained your gloves for no reason that I could think of. I asked for these, and whilst your linen still covered much of your hands, I could see the violinist's fingers on the left hand where gut strings had through the years scarred the pads at the extremities of the digits. I knew then without doubt that you were not Sir Henry, and the close proximity and evident collusion with Dr Watson told me the truth.'

Holmes was delighted with the dresser and his logical train of thought and quickly explained the reason for the impersonation. It was also necessary to swear him to secrecy; as the only person in the theatre that it would have been quite impossible to deceive.

Jennings was, we felt, a man to be trusted and he further promised to add to the realism of Holmes's role by spreading gossip concerning the sort of mood that 'Sir Henry' was in, as evidently was his habit.

Whilst the dresser was fetching some coffee we had the chance to discuss him.

'A shrewd man, Watson. He possibly missed his vocation, he should have been in my line of business.'

'Do you think he is trustworthy?'

'As far as that goes, Watson.'

'Surely he cannot be a suspect in your mind?'

'Everyone with the opportunity is a suspect. Remember, we may be looking for accessories as well as a murderer. But for the moment we have no alternative but to place our faith in Mr Jennings.'

And so it had to be, though at Holmes's muted suggestion I kept my eyes and ears open concerning the dresser.

But a very imminent crisis for Holmes was getting closer by the minute. I refused to believe that he had no sort of fear of taking on the double task, not only of impersonating Irving, but impersonating Irving playing Count Dracula! I realized that only his nerves of steel and histrionic abilities could get him through. Also I realized that he might need to rely heavily upon the prompter who sat in the prompt corner with the book of the play.

I managed to buttonhole the fellow, and make an excuse. 'Good evening. I am John Watson and as you may know I am Sir Henry's doctor.'

'I have seen you around lately, sir, and I knew that you were not just an admirer, but were filling some function.'

'How was the difference so clear?'

'Why, sir, those who call asking for

photographs or interviews for theatre group magazines are given only a few minutes of Sir Henry's time. I knew that you had to be a doctor or a solicitor or something of the kind.'

'Well, the fact is that Sir Henry has been suffering with a throat complaint for which I have found the perfect remedy.'

He looked at me strangely as he felt that there was little point in my informing him of a problem if I had already discovered the remedy. But he nodded understandingly as I continued. 'Regrettably, this excellent throat salve has an unfortunate tendency to produce drowsiness; for the next two or three performances Sir Henry will have little trouble with his voice but possibly a slight tendency to lose concentration. Therefore I beg that you give him even more attention than usual. If there are slight pauses which should not occur please do not put it down to a change in his way of interpretation, just give him the line with your usual excellent clarity.'

He nodded in complete agreement. 'Do not worry, Doctor, I will watch him like a hawk and listen for the slightest hesitation.'

I felt happier once I had consulted the prompter, but was still a great deal more uneasy than was Holmes himself. He said, 'Come, Watson, what can the audience do, short of thinking that Irving has given a performance below his usual standard?'

Holmes, as he left the dressing room to answer his 'call', suggested that I wait in that apartment until he should return. I was so nervous that I sent Jennings to sit in the Royal Box, that he might return at the interval to give me his assessment of Holmes's interpretation of Count Dracula. My nerves played havoc with me and for the whole hour I paced the dressing room.

When Jennings returned he smiled broadly and said, 'Well, Doctor, I do not think you need to worry further. Mr Holmes patently dried a couple of times, but in such a way that would only be obvious to someone in the know. The delivery of his lines was firm and clear, and although he lost position a few times he disguised the fact in ingenious ways. In other words, he carried it off!'

I had expected Holmes to return to the dressing room for the interval, but Jennings explained that the first interval was of short duration and that Holmes would change into another costume in the wings, as was Sir Henry's habit.

'I must go and assist him now, Doctor. There is a sort of canvas changing tent in the wings where the new costume awaits him.'

During the time that Jennings performed his valet-like duty as a theatrical dresser, I began to determine that I must see Holmes in the role. He had suggested that I remain in the dressing room, but when Jennings returned and therefore the apartment was safely occupied, I saw no reason why I should not creep down to the box and watch, at least for a short while.

My dear reader, I have, as you know, long admired my friend and colleague Sherlock Holmes. He is a splendid and loyal ally and a brilliant criminologist with an unbelievable knowledge of a thousand and one subjects. His faults are irritating, but few. Yes, my admiration for him knows no bounds, but I believe my regard for his talents reached a peak that autumn night at Brighton's Theatre Royal. His second big entrance occurred soon after the rise of the curtain upon Act Two. Although still adorned in a cloak with a raised collar he had changed the black tailed coat for a smoking jacket of crimson velvet. He raised his arms to turn his cloak to an appearance of batlike wings and said, 'Look into the mirror, dear lady, and tell me what you see?'

Miss Hargreaves said, 'Why, Count, I see myself in the dress that you admired so, also the splendid furnishings of your lovely home.'

'What else?'

'Nothing else . . . '

'Exactly! You do not see my own reflection, do you?'

'Why, no, I . . . '

Miss Hargreaves, realizing that she could not perceive the reflected image of Count Dracula, began to scream.

Holmes hesitated, then said, 'The children of the night who sing so sweetly have something to tell me.'

I alone realized that he was seeking his next line.

From that point on I was aware, whenever he made further appeal to the 'Children of the night' he was in fact appealing to be prompted! There were other points in that second act when although appearing not to need reminding he delivered long and effective speeches which I could not recall having heard from the lips of Irving. In other words, when Holmes not only dried but was unable to hear a prompt he fell back upon extemporizing speeches which not only kept within the context of the play but actually enhanced it.

The audience, unaware that they were hearing that which had been invented from necessity, were none the less appreciative of these speeches which to some measure improved the piece. There were murmurs of 'first class' and 'Irving was never better' as Holmes took his second act curtain. But I did not linger, taking myself through the pass door at the rear of the box and back to the star dressing room, knowing that the interval which preceded the final act was of a longer duration and that Holmes would have time to return to it. Jennings greeted me and I noticed that he was a trifle short of breath. I remarked upon this and he replied, 'The advancing years are taking their toll, Doctor, and were I an actor I would remark, 'I have grown quite breathless in Sir Henry's service'!'

I refrained from making the obvious remark to his beautifully delivered lines, 'But you are an actor, Jennings', for had we not learned already of his thespian origins. Then, as Holmes entered the room, Jennings departed to fetch coffee and I had a chance to confer with my friend. 'Holmes, I must congratulate you, for you were quite magnificent as Count Dracula. You pulled off the impersonation superbly. In fact, many patrons clearly thought that Sir Henry had surpassed himself.'

'They have called then, these patrons, to impart this praise?'

'Why no, I watched from the Royal Box.'

'Upon my word, you have left the dressing room where I believed that you would await my return. No matter, the fault was mine in believing that our liaison was long and close enough for you to realize this without need of instruction.'

I knew not quite how to reply but was spared by the return of Jennings with the coffee. As he poured this he remarked, 'Everyone is remarking about a first-class performance, sir,' — he dropped his voice — 'I do not believe anyone in the theatre had the faintest suspicion concerning the substitution.'

Holmes grunted. 'We have one more hurdle left, Jennings. I still have to pull it off for the third act. By the way, when did you hear these impressions.'

'Why just now, sir, when I fetched the coffee from the stalls café. You could not help but hear the comments. I have been here in this room save when I assisted you in the wings, as the Doctor will confirm.'

Sheepishly, I remarked, 'I watched from the box.'

He hesitated, and then said, 'Of course that is it, for you were not here, were you?'

I remember at this point thinking that it was fortunate that none of this was particularly important, for we had to the best of my knowledge been spared any further bizarre development. But then my false confidence was shattered by the entrance of the news-seller. Despite precautions to prevent intrusion he had climbed through the net. 'Here is your late *Argus*, Sir Henry . . . terrible murder in the Lanes!'

I prayed for a coincidence, but my hopes were dashed as I read the front-page story aloud to Holmes and Jennings.

'HORRIFIC MURDER IN HISTORIC LANES

'At about eight o'clock this evening a strange cloaked figure was observed to be retreating from the inert form of an elderly angler on his way home from the beach through one of Brighton's historic Lanes. The angler was found to be dead with wounds at his throat, and a strange pallor of his complexion. The first impression had to be that this was another of a series of murders with a similar set of circumstances. The main difference is that all of the previous killings, which the London press have come to refer to as 'The Vampire Murders', happened in the vicinity of London's Long Acre. The victim was found to have died from a broken neck despite the impression made by the throat wounds and evident pallor. These were caused in fact by a fork-like implement and the application of theatrical powder, just as with the Long Acre victims.

'Another similarity has to be mentioned, however reluctant your reporter may be to do so. The fact that Sir Henry Irving was presenting his dramatized version of Stoker's *Dracula* at the Lyceum which was but a stone's throw from Long Acre. The publicity surrounding the tragedies and their obvious comparison with the events of the play (especially in each case the sight of a retreating cloaked figure) had a detrimental effect upon the box office at the Lyceum. For this reason Sir Henry decided to transfer the play to Brighton's Theatre Royal. At first this appeared to clear up the matter as far as the actor was concerned with no more tragedies to report. However, when another murder near Long Acre occurred it was discovered that Sir Henry, far from being in Brighton playing Count Dracula, was at that point in the vicinity of the Lyceum where he had been discussing some business whilst an understudy replaced him at the Theatre Royal. *The Argus* is led to believe that at one point Sir Henry was helping the police with their enquiries. However, tonight he reappeared in his starring role at the Theatre Royal, Brighton, only to be plagued by this latest tragedy — once again within walking distance of his very presence. As far as your reporter can ascertain, Irving would have been actually upon the stage at the time of the murder. None the less the noble thespian must be greatly concerned with the series of coincidences(?) which must link his name with tragedy in the eyes of the public.

'We understand that Inspector Grant of the Sussex police is heading the investigations.

'Will Sir Henry Irving now abandon completely his production of *Dracula*, and if he does so, will this action see the end of these horrific murders with an evident Bram Stoker influence?'

I put down the paper, just as the call boy knocked upon the door and announced, 'Five minutes, Sir Henry!'

Holmes rose and said, 'Alas, I have to leave and cavort upon the stage! Watson, pray take this note to Lestrade.'

As he scribbled upon a sheet of paper and folded it, handing it to me I enquired, in some surprise, 'In London?'

'No, Watson. He awaits my instructions at the Desmond Hotel!'

As Holmes departed to continue in his new career, I took a cab to the Desmond Hotel and found the inspector actually in the lobby of that establishment. He seemed not especially surprised to see me, with my message. He scanned it quickly and then said, 'Righto, Dr Watson, I know what to do, but the less you know about it the better. Sometimes even a Scotland Yard man has to take certain liberties with the law!'

I knew better than to ask him for further enlightenment regarding his words. But as I made to leave, he called after me to enquire, 'How did the 'great actor' do at the Theatre Royal? Have the audience demanded their money back?'

I decided to treat his remark with the contempt it deserved. There was some difficulty which presented itself to me in gaining the hire of a cab to take me back to the theatre. There was a general air of emergency and when I got an elderly hansom, which would not even have kept its licence in London, the driver had great difficulty in manoeuvring through the streets. Indeed, even near the Theatre Royal itself, a good half-mile from the murder scene, there was some congestion. A police vehicle and obvious signs of press attention told their own story. I nudged my way through the crowd and past the stage doorkeeper who remarked to a police constable who stood guard, 'Sir Henry's doctor, he's all right!'

The constable muttered, 'He might be in need of a doctor by the time this night is over!'

Sir Henry in the person of Mr Sherlock Holmes was actually still upon the stage as I entered, and I estimated that he would be so for quite twenty minutes or thereabouts. But Jennings made a path for me through the persons who were crowding about the dressing room door. The dresser said, 'Doctor, please take a comfortable seat. I am going to close the door now and will open it only when Sir Henry returns.'

I realized that he had put emphasis upon the name lest we were overheard. Indeed, the whole atmosphere changed when Inspector Grant of the Sussex police demanded an entrance to the room which we could scarcely refuse. He was a plain-clothes detective, very alert and of military appearance despite his mufti. Quite a different character from Inspector Lestrade who represented a dying breed. I remembered not to mention Lestrade lest his presence in Brighton was supposed to be unknown. Indeed, I had taken such a clue from Lestrade's conspiratorial air at the Desmond. Grant nodded curtly. 'Grant, Sussex police. I understand, sir, that you are Sir Henry Irving's doctor?'

'Yes, at least I was recently called in to help with his vocal chords.'

'But you are not his regular physician. You are perhaps then a specialist in matters of the throat?'

I was weaving for myself a web in practising to deceive. But I tried to put as much truth into my words as I could in the hope that Holmes would quickly appear to give me some clue as to our plan of action. Would he continue his pretence of being Sir Henry Irving, or would he put all our cards upon the inspector's table?

'Well, I know quite a lot about problems of the kind; but mainly I am here to help Sir Henry through a difficult time.'

Feeling that the inspector could make of that what he would I was relieved that his questions were not beyond me to answer in a bland manner.

'Where were you, sir, at about eight o'clock this evening?'

'I was seated in a box in the theatre, watching Sir Henry as he played his part. I watched the whole of the second act from the box.'

'How much of the time during that second act was Sir Henry in full view of the audience?'

'Almost the whole time, and speaking for a great deal of it, which explains my concern for his voice.'

The inspector had been observing me closely. He asked, 'Dr Watson, have we met before? Your face seems somewhat familiar to me.'

I realized that he may have recognized me from one of Paget's illustrations in *The Strand*, but decided to continue my bluff. 'I do not recall having had the pleasure of meeting you, Inspector, but then I am not only a medic but an old soldier, and we tend to develop similarities. I am forever being mistaken for other military types.'

'Oh, quite so, no matter, I'm probably mistaken. Mind you, I have a very good memory for faces; useful in my job, what?'

To my intense gratification Holmes entered upon the scene at this point, thus reducing the responsibility that I felt the burden of.

He soon sized up the situation, quickly giving me the clue as to the avenue I should take. 'Ah, Inspector, I was told to expect to find you here. Irving, you know, and I believe your name is Grant?'

My relief was profound. I had done the right thing with Holmes keeping up his impersonation of the actor. The policeman looked at Holmes keenly. 'Sir Henry, I have long admired you on the stage. I could only wish that our meeting could have been under happier circumstances. Your voice seems to have held up well.'

Holmes was amazing in his continued offstage performance of 'The Great Actor'. He had his mannerisms and speech traits at his fingertips. 'Thank heaven, also my good friend, Dr Watson, what? He gave me valuable advice based on his many years' experience as a general practitioner in which he has always had success with vocal matters. Should have been a specialist, might have made some cash, what?'

The policeman seemed completely pacified. 'The doctor tells me that your part is a lengthy one and that you have been on stage throughout most of this evening, including the period between eight and half-past that hour?'

'Yes, with only a very few minutes between exits and entrances. The first interval I spent in the wings, in a dressing tent, preparing myself for Act Two. Inspector, I feel we could save much time by establishing that there is no way that I could have taken myself to the Lanes, murdered this poor old man and returned in time to make my next entrance.'

Holmes seemed to be walking a line between Irving's natural reactions and his own ironic feelings. The inspector, of course, noticed this very slight change of tone and replied, 'Sir Henry, I am not foolish enough to suppose that you had yourself committed this outrage any more than the London police could have believed such a thing at the time of the Long Acre murders. But, sir, the fact remains that there is no longer any doubt that there is some kind of connection between yourself and these crimes, and a connection too with the piece that you are playing. I have to decide if I believe that yours is an innocent link with the tragedies or if you are in some way causing them to occur. I do not myself believe this to be likely but I must cover all possibilities.'

Holmes, realizing that we were dealing with a man of intellect, dropped any ironic tone from his voice. 'Of course, Inspector. I take your point perfectly and will give you whatever co-operation I possibly can.'

I was not extremely concerned for my friend and the situation he was in. Mainly I was worried lest his deception concerning his identity should be discovered. What then would Inspector Grant make of things, especially taking the position of Henry Irving, the real Sir Henry who for all I knew could have been allowed by Lestrade to leave his home. I knew that he was not guilty of the murder, but how would such a circumstance look. Perjury could be just one of the charges brought against Sherlock Holmes.

As Grant left us for a moment or two for consultation with the constable at the door, Holmes turned to me and said, 'I believe I know what is going through your mind, Watson, but pray do not concern yourself. I am following a plan that I have devised.'

When Grant returned to us he said, 'Sir Henry, I would count it as a favour if I could use this dressing accommodation of yours as an interview room?'

Holmes chanced his arm at this point I felt. 'Inspector, you may do so with pleasure, on one condition.'

'Which is?'

'That Dr Watson and I might remain here throughout?'

I could see that the inspector was not entirely pleased with this suggestion. 'It would be frowned upon by my superiors, but as you are, how shall I say, the founder of the feast, I suppose it will do no harm.'

As it turned out Grant seemed glad to have Sir Henry present for the confirmation of various facts during the interviews, little knowing of course that he was dealing with Sherlock Holmes! Not unnaturally, Jennings was the first person to be interviewed, considering that he was already close at hand. He seemed honest and forthright in the way he answered the inspector's question. 'How long, Mr Jennings, have you served Sir Henry in the role of his dresser?'

'Just on twenty-five years, Inspector, as I think Sir Henry will confirm. I was an actor, looking for a part. I read for Sir Henry but he could not use me. Seeing that I was desperate he kindly offered me this post.'

The inspector brought matters nearer to the time of the tragedy. 'So, Mr Jennings, I believe you claim that you did not leave the theatre during this evening's performance.'

'That is correct.'

'Can anybody corroborate this claim?'

'Sir Henry, Dr Watson, maybe a few others.'

Holmes said, 'If I may, Inspector, Jennings attended me in my changing tent during the first interval.'

'After that?'

'I was, of course, on stage, but Dr Watson spoke with him at one point, I believe.'

I must have seemed a little bit sly as I said, 'I was watching Sir Henry from the box, but I, er, I did speak with Jennings from time to time . . . '

So sure was I of Jennings's innocence that I found myself verging on the borders of untruth and decided to say no more. The inspector, I believe, sympathized with my dilemma. 'Very well. Then I suppose others might be able to confirm your presence, Jennings. The stage door-keeper, for example.'

When Jennings showed signs of being somewhat sheepish, the inspector sent for the stage doorkeeper, a Mr Blair, who like most of his tribe presented a somewhat portly and beery appearance. He spoke rather breathlessly. 'Why yes, sir, Mr Jennings went out at about four or five minutes after eight.'

Jennings broke in curtly, 'But George, I returned a couple of minutes later . . . you remember? I had only slipped out to get some coffee.'

I was forced in fairness to say, 'But Jennings, I thought you always got the coffee from the café in the stalls?'

The dresser was uncomfortable. 'Oh, that's right. I must have slipped out for the newspaper. But anyway, George must have seen me return.'

The stage doorkeeper said, 'I can't say for sure. I was reading me paper, but I'm sure you returned if you say so, Mr Jennings.'

Rather to my surprise Grant seemed to tire of the subject and told Jennings that he could go. 'But do not leave the theatre, Mr Jennings. Oh, and perhaps you could send up Mr Mornington.'

Charles Mornington I had observed to be an excellent actor playing Van Helsing with great skill and charisma. Offstage he was also a pleasant enough fellow. He volunteered all of his movements during the period between eight and half-past, being bright enough to realize that this was the information mainly required of him. His several short appearances, entrances and exits during that time made it clear that he could scarcely have stepped outside the Theatre Royal let alone journey to the Lanes and back. But Grant seemed almost uninterested in this information. Instead he seemed to be testing Mornington's attitude toward Sir Henry.

'How long have you known Sir Henry Irving, Mr Mornington?'

'Many years, Inspector. We have worked together many times, largely through Sir Henry's kindness in always considering me when a suitable part crops up. I would say we have known each other for ten or twelve years.'

But I noticed that when he said this he was studying Holmes keenly. I remembered that Lady Irene had given us the impression that the two men had been acquainted for somewhat longer and I hoped that Holmes would remember this.

Fortunately he did. 'Rather longer than that, George: nearer twenty years.'

'Has it really been as long as that?'

Mornington owned up to a mistake which I felt had really been meant as a test. I was now deeply concerned that he had seen through Holmes's disguise. This would scarcely have been surprising, but he seemed not to press his suspicion.

Grant asked him a few more questions and then asked him if he would send in Miss Hargreaves. This lady proved to have no difficulty in corroborating her movements during the time which was of importance and seemed to have no suspicions whatever concerning the identity of 'The Great Actor'. This was also the case with Miss Mountjoy, though she gave me an uncomfortable moment when she leaned over to Holmes and said, 'Henry, you did not half make a meal of it when you bit my neck tonight! Those fangs are sharp . . . gently, duckie, like you usually do it, tomorrow night!'

The last of the cast (and I was suddenly struck with how very few actors were required save for a few supernumeraries) was Ashley Barrington, who of all of them was the most likely to be identified as an actor when away from the theatre, I felt. He was somewhat affected in his style of speech, yet I had to admit that he had made a first-class job of impersonating the strange character of the insect-devouring 'Renfrew'. Like the rest of the cast he could account for his presence in the theatre during the entire performance. But he bore out Lady Irene's impression of him when he appeared to wish to make irritations for Sir Henry.

'Your new doctor must be doing your voice a power of good, Henry, for I notice you have sent your understudy away, or given him the night off.'

After he had left, Grant confronted

Holmes with this point. 'Was that not rather daring of you, Sir Henry, to send your understudy home when you were having such trouble with your voice as Mr Barrington remarked?'

Holmes gave his best Sir Henry Irving shrug, saying, 'It was part of Watson's treatment. He insisted on it!'

I could have slaughtered Holmes for landing me with a tricky question to answer. Fortunately I managed what I felt was a fair and ingenious comment. 'You know, Inspector, I think I can tell you in confidence that Sir Henry has a problem with his voice that is not so much physical as mental. There is nothing wrong with his mind, but he has been suffering through lack of confidence following a quite mild sore throat. I decided to give him my support, and part of the treatment was to send the deputy home. I felt that if Sir Henry had felt that the man was there to replace him, he could have imagined a return of his throat trouble.'

Inspector Grant looked at me long

and hard, eventually saying, 'You are indeed the most versatile of medical men, Doctor: a throat specialist, an expert on problems of the mind; is there no end to your talents? Yet still an ordinary GP! You really should have more letters after your name.'

Holmes jumped in quickly, saying, 'Dr Watson is a family friend, I trust him and rely on his judgement more than I would any fancy specialist. I believe now that he was right when he said that my throat trouble stemmed from my imagination. He has established that there is really nothing wrong with my throat!'

He gave a wonderful performance of a man prone to have imaginary ailments. His hand shook and he turned to me. 'Look, Doctor, that shaking has started again.'

I played my part. 'Now, Sir Henry, we have been through all that . . . there is no medical reason for you to shake. Just calm yourself. It is just this business of the murders getting at you again.'

Grant seemed to swallow all this, or if he did not he obviously did not think it important. Several other people were interviewed, but the interviews stopped short at questioning the regular theatre staff or persons in general who would appear to have no connection with Sir Henry Irving. At length he said, 'Well, Sir Henry, it grows late and I see no harm now in sending everyone home.'

To my surprise, Holmes studied Sir Henry's gold watch and said, 'Yet I have not finished with everyone yet. I know the hour is late but I will have to exercise my right to hold a meeting upon the stage as I do from time to time.'

Grant muttered, 'At this hour?'

'Circumstances alter cases; such a meeting is necessary.'

5

The Midnight Meeting

The theatrical set which represented the interior of Castle Dracula took on an even more eerie appearance under the theatre worklight as compared with its normal stage illumination. The curtains were drawn apart but only the stage was lit, with the auditorium being in all but total darkness save for the faint glow of one or two safety lamps. Upon the stage there sat, in a semicircle, the entire cast, plus one or two others whose presence Holmes had demanded for his meeting, in his role as Sir Henry Irving.

As we walked down the centre aisle, or rather felt our way down it, Holmes told me to take my seat in the front of the stalls, next to Inspector Grant and the *Argus* reporter who, to my surprise, had been permitted to remain. As I seated myself, Holmes walked through the pass door and then out on to the stage. He showed us his back for a moment as he turned to bow to the seated actors and others. Then he proceeded to talk to them and to us, turning to face whomsoever he addressed.

'Ladies and gentlemen of the company, Inspector Grant, Mr Dobson of the *Argus*, Dr Watson *et al.*, I feel I owe you all an explanation and indeed an apology for making this midnight meeting call. I called it for a variety of reasons but first because I owe those of you in the theatre a full and detailed account of the events of the past couple of weeks.

'When I decided to stage *Dracula* I did so with an enthusiasm that I doubt I would have felt had I realized what might occur through its production. I need hardly tell you how horrified I was by those terrible murders in the area quite close to the Lyceum. Whilst I was not responsible for these terrible crimes, and indeed could not have been through the circumstances of time and location, yet I felt a guilt in case my portrayal or the very presentation of the play had caused these bizarre events. With the sighting in each case of a retreating cloaked figure, the throat wounds and the pallor of the victims made a link appear positive. After the second killing I had all but decided to take off the play and hope that it would make an end to these tragic events. But then I considered my responsibilities to you, my fellow actors. My dears, you had each made provision in your lives upon the expectation of a long run of the sort normally associated with the name Irving. To put it bluntly you have all, I know, made it clear that you will not be available for other productions for at least a year.'

There was some muttering and nodding of heads among the players. Sir Henry Irving continued, 'Knowing therefore not which way to turn I decided to consult that eminent detective, Mr Sherlock Holmes.

He and his colleague, Dr John Watson, were so very kind and helpful . . . '

I started. I wondered why Holmes had decided to put me into this revealed position, especially in front of Inspector Grant (who by the way I sensed turning to face me, even in the almost complete blackout of the auditorium). The narration continued. 'We decided between us that rather than close the production down I should try moving it to the provinces as an experiment. This historic south coast location was chosen and Holmes was kind enough to send his colleague to watch events here whilst he remained in London. After the first night or so I confess I became complacent and believed that the change of location had ended the whole tragic business. I decided to give my understudy a chance to appear for me whilst I feigned a minor illness and took myself off to the Lyceum where I had business to handle, not unconnected with the possibility of a return to that location when I could be sure that it was safe to do so.

'Unfortunately, or tragically, the murderer struck again in the area of the Lyceum, making the finger of guilt seem to point to this old thespian in particular, rather than the production in general. Dear friends, I confess that on this one occasion I was unable to prove a presence at any particular place during the vital period involved. I was arrested, yes. I can tell you now, that I, Henry Irving, actually languished in a police cell, though thanks largely to Mr Holmes's intervention I was spared the ignominy of becoming an actual convict. Through his friendship with Inspector Lestrade, a splendid fellow from Scotland Yard, I was allowed to return to my home and absolutely no publicity resulted from this unfortunate occurrence.

'Mr Holmes, good fellow that he is, decided to allow my return to Brighton, after consultation with Inspector Lestrade, just so long as Dr

Watson was close to me at all times. Watson can, of course, vouch for all of my movements and for those of most of my colleagues during the vital time span of tonight's regrettable, latest tragedy. I believe my dresser, Mr Jennings, was found to have left the theatre, on the pretext of fetching coffee which he could have obtained within the building. But his absence was far too short for him to have been able to have taken himself to the Lanes and back again. In any case, Jennings has been with me for a great many years and is, if I might say so, beyond reproach, as in fact are the rest of you, which makes it obvious that it is someone from outside the theatre, and I use the word in its all-encompassing sense, who is responsible.'

At this point a diversion of an extraordinary kind took place.

'We know all about ourselves, but more important, who, sir, are you?' These words were uttered by Ashley

Barrington who jumped to his feet and pointed an accusing finger at Sir Henry in a manner so typical of an actor. I started, fearing that Barrington had penetrated Holmes's disguise. His words and behaviour in the dressing room had caused me some concern in that direction.

'Why, my dear Ashley, surely you have known me long enough to make such a question cause us to doubt your sanity?'

If Barrington's actions and words had raised all eyebrows this was to be as nothing compared to his next utterances and movements. He extended the fingers of both hands and with them grasped those extremely prominent eyebrows which were so beloved of cartoonists. He tugged at them as if expecting them to be removed with a certain amount of force. (I must admit that I expected as much myself!) When the only result was a yell of pain from the great actor, Barrington backed away in some surprise. But he quickly recovered, saying, 'So, an imposter has been found with eyebrows like Henry's! This man is an imposter; he is an incredibly similar deputy who played Dracula this evening, perhaps leaving Irving free to have committed the ghastly crime in the Lanes after all.'

I knew not what to expect at this point. Would Holmes, having had his disguise seen through, now make a clean breast of things or would he brazen it out? I knew him to be capable of doing even this.

Instead the actor said, 'Barrington, I will prove to you who I am, but I can assure you that you have trodden the boards with me for the last time. Jennings, be good enough to fetch a sponge and a bowl of warm water!'

Whilst we awaited the return of the dresser, I wondered just what Holmes had in his mind. Was he about to reveal himself, sans rouge, sans nose putty, sans everything, and if so, why?

Barrington peered down into the blackness of the stalls and said,

'Inspector Grant, I hope you have observed all that has happened and will continue to observe what next occurs. Why, ask yourself, did Sir Henry send away his regular understudy and send this man to the theatre in his place? Obviously the usual man could not deceive at close quarters. He has found a man who looks almost exactly like him when using a suitable make-up. This fact will be revealed. Whilst on the stage with him this evening in a stronger light than this, aye and in the dressing room, I could see that his nose had been built up and even offstage and having cleaned off his make-up he had applied another for close observation!'

Jennings reappeared with a bowl and sponge, and dutifully washed the great actor's face, having first spread a towel across his shirt front and dress vest. I wondered if, being aware of the deception, that he had invented a way of doing this without producing any seen result. He was, after all, accomplished in his work in the application and removal of theatrical cosmetics. But I will say that he seemed quite startled himself when no trace of grease paint or powder appeared upon the sponge. Puzzled, he passed the damp sponge to Miss Hargreaves who also tried to take the visage of Sir Henry Irving from the so-called imposter. It was soon quite clear that it was indeed Sir Irving who stood before us.

Barrington spluttered his apology. 'Henry, my dear fellow, I was mistaken! I should have known that you would not have been party to a deception of the kind. I say, I hope this little incident will not affect our friendship, or our professional connections?'

Sir Henry Irving was obviously very angry. 'Barrington, I was not aware that there ever was friendship between us. I have employed you many times because you are a first-rate actor. I shall have to think very carefully before I ever employ you again.'

Ashley Barrington cringed. 'Do you know, it is rather funny really, but as you stood there, I genuinely thought you to be an imposter. I even thought that you might have been that detective fellow, Sherlock Holmes, at one point. He doesn't seem to have been much help to you. I mean, where is he when he could help you the most?'

My friend Sherlock Holmes had already proved himself a fine actor, now he demonstrated the fine sense of drama that was his trademark. As if in answer to Barrington's words, he walked out on to the stage, dressed in his own clothes and holding a fully charged meerschaum in his right hand. An extra chair was brought for Irving who sat down gratefully, having sustained an extremely fine oration to rival anything that he had performed as part of a play. He smiled and inclined his head to the detective as if to say, 'Your turn now'.

Holmes held us on tenterhooks as he lit the pipe with a vesta. He was as formal in his words as had been the great actor before him. 'Ladies and gentlemen of the company, Inspector, Watson, Jennings and whoever else it may concern, I will make an explanation of recent events. I owe this to you, most of you having been at least considered as suspects. When I use the word I should perhaps change it to accessory, for none of you as far as I can see had the opportunity to commit the murders which I have been investigating.'

Some fidgeting of those seated upon the stage appeared to be with relief as its cause. Holmes continued, 'I was looking for some cause and personage not of an obvious nature and this in mind I paid particular attention to memorabilia, framed and otherwise, shown to me by Sir Henry and Lady Irene. I was looking for a name or a face that might give me some clue. I believe I found both.

'You know, the human mind is a wondrous thing: capable of prompting its owner for good or evil. As for evil, this is also something which is divided from good by a hair-thin line. Actors and some other celebrities, but chiefly actors, attract persons who admire them not just for their performances but also for themselves as people. These persons are the actor's chief allies, for they watch for his name if he is a favourite performer of theirs, that they be sure to purchase seats at the theatre to see his latest vehicle. The actor therefore depends upon having such admirers, but there are sometimes those among them who go a little bit too far. They will do anything to meet their idol, talk to him, and they will cover the walls of their abodes with his likeness. This, whilst it may sound a little extreme to most of us, is still harmless enough. But there are those among them who become a little unhinged, and demand that their idol should return their interest in some way. Then should he cause them some slight, such is their state of mind that their adulation will suddenly turn to hatred!

'After many years of contact with

such a mixed crowd of wrongdoers I can recognize many categories of them from their characteristics, sometimes even from their facial expressions. As I looked through Sir Henry's remarkable collection of pictures covering his work over a period of half a century, I began to recognize one face that appeared in any picture where the public were involved, such as outside a theatre after an opening night. Yes, he was always there and in the earlier pictures he had that open-faced admiration of the others. Eventually, however, in later pictures he seemed to have taken on a sullen, almost evil, expression. Why would such a man, whose admiration seemed to have changed to some form of dislike, continue to frequent the places where this famous actor appeared? Love had turned to hate, and it was only a matter of time before he would actually attempt to harm his one-time idol.'

I could see now, as a medical man, just where Holmes's train of thought had taken him. I, too, had seen those pictures, but I suppose I had just not been looking for the same things as was my friend. Come to think of it, he was looking for everything and anything which might throw light upon the darkness of our investigation. I noticed that the words had struck some sort of chord with most of the actors. Miss Hargreaves particularly was nodding and assuming an expression of complete understanding.

Holmes continued, 'The killings in the Long Acre area, these were performed evidently pointlessly for there was no similarity in the victims; but there was something terribly theatrical in the pretence, obvious pretence, of the connection with a vampire. This would suggest someone wishing to harm Sir Henry. Of course, they must have realized that he could prove his presence at the Lyceum at the time of the killings, but they no doubt appreciated that the whole implication would be very bad for business in the theatre box office.

'When the play was moved to Brighton the murderer moved here too. But when Sir Henry made his one mistake in leaving his understudy to play and visiting London without informing me, the stalking fiend knew his movements and did likewise. This was the one killing that would not have happened, at least not in that place. But when Inspector Lestrade showed such understanding, allowing Sir Henry to return to Brighton, the killer followed him yet again. At this stage I had but a face, a tuning fork and some theatrical powder to watch for. A name emerged later.'

I started in my seat in the stalls. Was Holmes going to completely ignore his great impersonation in giving this explanation?

'On our return to Brighton' — ah, so Holmes implied the three of us — 'I noticed an itinerant violinist playing outside the stage door. Watson had mentioned him in passing in one of his reports and this returned to my mind. In tossing a coin into his fiddle case I noticed a tuning fork, plus some grey powder. Of course, resin!'

I could not help but interrupt at this point. 'Holmes, would these things not be expected to be found in a violinist's case?'

'True, Watson, but perhaps not in the case of a man who played so badly as to be all but asking for money under false pretences. I alerted Lestrade to have him watched at all times, and arrested if and when it was apt.'

It was Charles Mornington who enquired, 'Forgive me, Mr Holmes, but you promised you could give us a name as well as a face. For I imagine the violinist must have reminded you of the face in the photographs.'

Holmes nodded. 'Yes, Mr Mornington. I could see in the features of the fiddling derelict something of the face in the pictures. He was also wearing the expensive shoes which could have been those that made the prints in Long

Acre. Doubtless, though, they could easily have been given to him by someone more fortunately placed. Mr Jennings, I have noticed that you wear the particular make of shoe.'

The dresser gasped. 'Why, I do like a good shoe, sir, but then so do many others.'

Holmes looked back to Mornington. 'You asked for a name, sir, and I will give you one. Jennings.'

The dresser looked around in help-less fear, as if looking for an avenue of escape. 'Surely you are not accusing me of being a murderer?'

Holmes looked accusing as he said, 'You know, Mr Jennings, that I am not! I was asked for a name and I gave it. Robert Jennings is a name which Sir Henry would have noticed had he dealt with his own correspondence. But usually Lady Irving or a secretary would deal with the almost daily requests for photographs, or personal meetings and interviews. Had the name Jennings been so often presented to him he would have soon realized the coincidence or otherwise with the name of his dresser. But these things were dealt with, so that the great actor was free to devote all his time to his craft. Over the past twenty years it appears that many communications have been received from a Robert Jennings: early examples being polite and indeed full of adulation. Later ones were more demanding, and finally recent examples in the nature of threats, unsigned but in a handwriting known and recognized by those dealing with them. I suggest, Mr George Jennings, that your brother, Robert Jennings, deserves to be branded as a prime suspect for the role of the murderer we have been seeking: the individual referred to by the journalists as the 'Long Acre Vampire'.'

George Jennings hung his head as he replied, 'I have tried to drive such a belief from my mind, yet I suppose I have known for some time that this had to be so. It is as you have said, Mr Holmes: Robert went through a number of stages in connection with Sir Henry. At first he merely admired Britain's greatest actor, as did so many more. Then it started to become an obsession; in fact I think there was a point where he actually believed that he *was* Sir Henry Irving. Wherever Sir Henry and I were, Robert would eventually appear in the crowd outside the theatre, or hanging around near the entrance of a restaurant, even outside hotels where Sir Henry stayed. I was fortunately able to prevent Robert from any actual confrontation, but through the last year or two I fancied he had learned to hate his idol and was gradually becoming a danger to him. Of course, you are right that he has taken to the role of a street musician turning up wherever Sir Henry appears. He is to be pitied, Mr Holmes, for his obsession with Sir Henry has cost him his job, his marriage, even his self-respect. I have done my best to keep the two of them apart, and now I have I believe told you all that I know. I will only add that I hope that your suspicions regarding the Long Acre murders and the Lanes' killing are unfounded.'

Holmes nodded with appreciation. 'I admire your frankness, Mr Jennings. It will, of course, be up to a higher authority than mine to determine your brother's guilt or innocence.' Holmes peered down into the darkness of the auditorium and addressed Inspector Grant. 'By the way, my dear Grant, with Inspector Lestrade of Scotland Yard being on the spot and given the opportunity, I trust you will forgive the fact that he has arrested Robert Jennings?'

Grant grunted before he spoke. 'Well, strictly speaking, I should have made the arrest, but under these extraordinary circumstances, I am willing to co-operate with Scotland Yard.'

I had seldom heard of such respectful giving way by a high-ranking policeman. Usually the rivalry between the various constabularies is keen. But all such considerations went from my head when Lestrade walked out onto the stage with his prisoner. Robert Jennings stood there, looking gaunt and without hope in such dramatic lighting. He said, 'Well, Sir Henry, you have finally destroyed me, just as I had planned to destroy you.'

Irving jumped to his feet and said, 'You have destroyed yourself, sir, for I did you no harm.'

'No harm, when you consistently turned away my admiring friendship for so long? I gave you every chance to treat me as you should have. Finally I realized that I had wasted the greater part of my adult life in my worship for he whom I considered must be the greatest actor of all time. All I wanted from you was a kind word, a letter, a meeting even. Well, I admit that I committed those killings in Long Acre, in order to spoil your play at the Lyceum. I drove you out of there, didn't I, and if you had not called in Sherlock Holmes, Scotland Yard would be none the wiser!'

It was Holmes who next spoke. 'You admit, then, that you are the murderer?'

Robert Jennings shrugged. 'Oh yes, there is not much point in my denying it, after hearing what you have had to say. Inspector Lestrade was kind enough to allow me to hear you from the darkness of the wings! But I want to make it clear that I admit only to the killings near Long Acre.'

Would the drama never cease, for at this point Lestrade beckoned like some militant stage producer, and from the gloom of the opposite wing from which he and Robert Jennings had entered, there came forth an officer of the Sussex constabulary who laid a hand upon the shoulder of the hapless fellow and having made the usual formal caution, clapped handcuffs upon him and marched him from our view.

Holmes then addressed Lestrade. 'Inspector, I feel sure that the confession we have all heard made this arrest by a member of the local force justified?'

Lestrade nodded affably. 'Oh yes, I feel sure that Inspector Grant will be delighted to get the credit.'

To my amazement he winked at Grant who scarcely suppressed a snigger. Yet I was myself far from amused, for dark thoughts had started to enter my mind. Despite our long friendship and the presence of so many others, I felt I simply had to voice my feelings.

'You knew, or at least firmly suspected, that this Robert Jennings was the murderer of several unfortunate victims in the vicinity of the Lyceum well before this evening, yet you made no step to have him apprehended until yet another terrible slaughter of an innocent person had taken place!'

Holmes was grave but calm. 'I needed the confession that you heard from Jennings in order to have his arrest effected by the local police. I could have had him arrested earlier, but needed the establishment of facts that our little drama of this evening has supplied.'

Hardly could I believe the evidence of my own ears. I felt forced to add, with what I felt to be justifiable anger, further accusation. 'Upon my word, so you stage-managed events in a manner which you hoped would enable you to grab the murderer red-handed. Yet this you seem to have been unable to do, so you staged a foolish charade instead. It is all quite unworthy of you, Holmes!'

'It was all necessary, Watson . . . '

I raised my voice in anger against Sherlock Holmes, the only time I had done so during our long association. I had often enough chided or rebuked him, but never before in genuine rage. I answered his words. 'You should try telling the angler's widow that it was necessary!'

Holmes's reply seemed to me at that time to be idiotic enough to suggest some loss of his intellect. 'What angler, Watson?'

I controlled myself enough to reply, 'The angler who was murdered in the Lanes of Brighton, this very evening.'

What next was said by Sherlock Holmes only fuelled my previous feelings concerning his mind. 'No one was murdered in Brighton this evening.' He looked at his watch. 'Or rather I should now say *last* evening, for it has long passed the witching hour.'

'But . . . but Holmes, what can you mean? Have I not seen the whole affair reported in the *Evening Argus*?'

Holmes chuckled, he actually chuckled. 'Our friends at the *Argus* were most co-operative when I asked them to print a dozen copies of their paper with a bogus news item. Really, Watson, surely you must realize the impossibility of the item finding its way so quickly into the evening newspaper? I had hoped it might deceive others, but scarcely dared to hope that you might be taken in by it. Obviously the item had been set up and printed some hours earlier.'

I was still bewildered, as were some of the others. Charles Mornington enquired, 'Please do not tell me that you deceived Inspector Grant of the Sussex constabulary with a bogus murder?'

The actor pointed dramatically in the direction where he believed Inspector Grant to be seated in the dark. Sherlock Holmes asked, 'To which Inspector Grant do you refer?'

The answer came swiftly, 'The Inspector Grant mentioned in the *Argus*, the Inspector Grant who is sitting in the stalls!'

Holmes chuckled as he replied, 'We have already established that the *Argus* carried a bogus report; no such officer exists, and the man to whom you refer is a member of your own profession.'

'An actor?'

'Exactly. Mr Cyril Chambers is a colleague of Sir Henry's, good enough to accept a one-night engagement. Thank you, Mr Chambers, for a splendid performance.'

The person I had taken for Inspector Grant replied, 'It was a pleasure, Mr Holmes. In fact I quite enjoyed it, and I'm so glad that I was convincing in the role.'

Sir Henry interjected, 'My dear Cyril, I would engage you to play a detective inspector at any time.'

Lestrade also had a word to say to the actor. 'Well done, Chambers. I found you most convincing and you can count on my recommendation at any time. In the end it all worked out, a bit of play acting that secured a confession, without which the local force could scarcely have acted. I had to take a chance in apprehending Jennings, being outside of my own jurisdiction and without the documentation I would have required to break the rules, so to speak. But I must tell you that without the help of Sherlock Holmes, I might never have brought this satisfactory conclusion about.'

There was a general sharp intake of breath, as almost everyone present gasped at this typical Lestrade statement. But Sherlock Holmes was unsurprised, untroubled and indeed sanguine as he said, 'Always glad to be of help, Lestrade.'

The hour was late, or early, whichever way you care to look at it; yet there were several questions to be answered. Most of the assembled company had departed when Jennings, the dresser, asked, 'Am I also to be arrested, Inspector Lestrade?'

The inspector spoke kindly in reply. 'I think not; for the moment anyway, but possibly not at all. However, you do have some involvement, however unintentional, and I am fairly certain that you will eventually be called upon to give evidence in court. I am a policeman and not a lawyer, but it is my view that any charge against yourself would be of a minor nature. But as for your brother, Robert Jennings, it is fair to warn you that he may well be for the drop!'

Whilst not wishing to raise false hopes for Jennings, I ventured to say, 'It may not come to that, for any judge and jury would surely take into account the murderer's state of mind.'

But Holmes thought that this might be a trifle optimistic. 'These were ghastly crimes, well planned and carried out quite without heed of cruelty, simply to attempt the ruination of a respected and blameless celebrity. Don't forget that an insanity plea would depend upon the co-operation of a police doctor. That particular race of medics is not renowned for its sympathetic attitude toward modern thought upon the balance of the mind.'

I felt really sorry for Jennings, especially when Sir Henry Irving, rather untypically I thought, said, 'Jennings, I fear that despite our long association I must dispense with your services. I will, of course, pay you a not inconsiderable sum which should keep you whilst you seek other employment. I appreciate your divided loyalties, but I fear I could never forget that you offered me no sort of warning.'

The dresser said, 'I quite understand, Sir Henry, and in my own defence, I will only say that I would certainly have warned you had I felt that you were yourself in any sort of danger.'

Jennings departed without receiving further reply from the actor. It was clear that Sir Henry was saddened by what he had felt he had to do, but later he cheered considerably as he remarked to my friend, 'A great little drama we performed between us tonight, my dear Holmes, what? Old Barrington's face was a study when my eyebrows refused to budge, eh? Good thing he didn't try pulling my hair!'

I said, 'I was completely taken in, I thought you were Holmes at that moment! Just when and how was the transposition effected?'

It was Holmes who answered. 'Oh, come Watson, we all walked through an all but unlit theatre. A herd of elephants could have lurked unseen in the auditorium, let alone one distinguished and identically clothed actor!'

I said, 'You memorized and declaimed very well, just as Holmes would have done himself.'

Irving replied, 'My dear fellow, I was always what is known in our business as a 'quick study'!'

6

Curtain Calls

The yellow press and even the establishment papers made much of the 'Long Acre Vampire' when Robert Jennings came to trial. For come to trial he did, having been pronounced perfectly sane by several doctors. His brother, George, fared better on that score, as you will learn from this final chapter of my account of one of the most bizarre cases ever to involve Sherlock Holmes. Bizarre it was, to the very last.

Sherlock Holmes decided that he would not attend the trial at the Old Bailey save when he was required to give evidence. 'I can do little other than tell the truth now, Watson, and even that will be far from helpful in saving Robert Jennings from the gallows. Your own evidence, as a medical man, could, I feel, have slightly more effect in that direction. However, even so, he was not your patient and you can only give an opinion based upon commonsense and knowledge of past cases.'

The most extraordinary circumstance surrounding the affair came when we learned that Sir Henry Irving himself had engaged a famous barrister, Sir Oswald Carrington, to defend Robert Jennings. This news astounded us, especially when we remembered all the ruses with which he had collaborated in order to effect a confession and subsequent arrest.

But he gave us his reason when he called at 221B Baker Street to thank Holmes for his successful pursuance of his case. 'My dear Holmes, and Watson, my dear chap, this whole unfortunate affair has given me a lesson that I will never forget.'

Holmes replied, 'Come, there can be no blame attached to yourself, Sir Henry.'

'No blame? Oh yes, I think I have much to answer for.'

'Such as?'

'Such as taking my dear admiring public for granted and ignoring the fact that there could be among them those who are to be more pitied than blamed. I should have agreed to meet Robert Jennings at that stage where he was merely a nuisance rather than a menace. I could perhaps have spared several lives had I made a friend of him.'

I said, 'I doubt it, Sir Henry, for his mind was going through a number of dangerous changes. It is possible that such involvement with him might have placed your own life in danger rather than merely your reputation.'

He nodded. 'None the less, in the future I will not risk my own difficulties being thrust onto others. I will cultivate the company of any admirer who demands it. I have studied the faces of those who appear in those stage-door photographs which helped Holmes to trace the killer. I have realized that they could all have been made so much happier had I taken the trouble to stop and chat with each of them. Even a few kind words could have made such a difference.'

I could tell Holmes was tiring of the topic when he said, 'Come, Sir Henry, you have done all you could be expected to do. The chance of another so-called admirer taking his adulation to such a stage is remote. As for immediate concerns, Robert Jennings is certain to hang, despite your, in my opinion, misplaced provision of a barrister. But you might well be able to help his brother should any charge be made against him. He has been of good character in your employ for a great many years, which would be in his favour.'

The actor said, 'I will do all I can for him, short of reinstating him as my dresser. I must have those about me that I can trust.'

★ ★ ★

As for the trial itself, it lingered on for many weeks, being extremely complicated, dealing as it did with a number of victims and aspects. During my own evidence I did my very best to suggest that Robert Jennings was bordering upon insanity if not in fact stark raving mad. I was rebuked by the judge once or twice and told that my professional opinion concerning the accused prisoner's state of mind was not being solicited. Holmes, when called upon, also tried to imply that Jennings was insane with similar rebuke. But my friend had enough to worry about in giving his evidence without dwelling upon that particular. It was difficult enough for himself, Sir Henry Irving and Sir Oswald Carrington, let alone the prosecutor, to clarify the events that had surrounded the 'Long Acre Vampire'.

Sir Oswald had more success is exemplifying the good character and hapless position of the murderer's brother. He cleverly suggested that any allegations that he could have made would have been thought to be purely the fruits of an overactive imagination. He received serious rebuke, but it was clear that no further action would be taken against him.

The jury were out for a long time which led me to wonder if the matter of Jennings's sanity or lack of it had played quite a large part in their deliberations. However, they were faced with an admission of multiple murder by a man who in the dock had seemed alarmingly sane. Further, the judge had instructed them to simply consider if the accused had actually committed the crimes.

'Have you considered your verdict?'

'We have, M'lud.'

The age-old ritual was enacted.

'Do you find the accused guilty or not guilty?'

'Guilty, M'lud!'

I had witnessed murder trials before and had seen the judge put on the black cap and pronounce those sepulchral words which end with, ' . . . and hung by the neck until you are dead . . . '

This time a special kind of chill ran through me, for I had been close to the whole bizarre episode. But Holmes managed to preserve his usual sang-froid at the result which he had known to be inevitable. He had only reacted when Robert Jennings, asked if he had anything to say by the judge, had spoken up strongly, 'Children of the night, how sweetly they sing!'

Holmes turned to me and remarked, 'Jennings may have lost his reason, but certainly not his nerve.'

★ ★ ★

During the days that followed, spanning the conclusion of the trial and the actual execution, I found it difficult to dismiss the matter from my mind. However, Holmes showed no sign of dwelling upon the matter for he had a few outstanding cases to bring to a conclusion pending his imminent retirement. During the excitement that had surrounded the 'Long Acre Vampire' murders, I had quite forgotten the finality that was in Holmes's determination to finish his career whilst at the very height of his power mentally, and whilst young enough in body to take on a fresh calling. The sitting room at 221B was beginning to look like one's mental picture of behind the scenes at a large post office with so many parcels and packages destined for transportation to Fowlhaven, a few miles short of Eastbourne in Sussex.

But even Sherlock Holmes was affected when the morning of the execution dawned. We were both up, almost from dawn, and then to our very great surprise Mrs Hudson entered to announce, 'Sir Henry Irving.'

We were both surprised but welcomed our early-morning guest as well as the circumstances would allow. A space was cleared of Holmes's parcels so that coffee and rolls could be served; it seeming too early for the offer of a breakfast to be made. But Sir Henry was not able to take advantage of Mrs Hudson's baking, and he settled for the hot black liquid which sends those darts of energy into the brain. He hardly needed to give a reason for this extraordinarily early and unannounced visit, for the three of us had shared an incredibly strange series of experiences and we sensed that he felt that we must share the final curtain. He did not need to express this, but rather he said, 'I knew that I would find you up and about, even at this ungodly hour. For myself, I have not slept for a week, save in fits and starts.'

Sherlock Holmes, having sampled his coffee, sent his brain further darts by means of strong tobacco. He finished lighting his pipe and said, 'My dear Sir Henry, if I allowed my mind to operate in such an undisciplined fashion, I would never sleep at all. Watson may be about at such an hour for the same reason as yourself, but I am simply intent on getting on with the preparations for my impending move to

Sussex. It is incredible the amount of bric-a-brac that one collects during all but twenty years of one's life. I use the word collect in the general sense of course, for I have never made a deliberate collection of anything, save for practical or professional purposes. I do not collect newspaper cuttings, they simply accrue, as do chemicals and the equipment to make use of them. You might glance at a shelf and imagine me to be a collector of tobacco pipes, yet all of them are in regular use: each of them will correspond with a different mood of mine.'

I felt like asking Holmes which pipe he would select to smoke whilst awaiting to hear of the execution of a man whom he had helped bring to book; a man who belonged in an asylum rather than in a condemned cell. However, I could see for myself that he had chosen the well-worn and partially blackened clay which I felt sure he had simply picked up because it had come to hand rather than through any process of selection.

The noble thespian raised his eyes heavenwards and spoke in the sepulchral tones of the gloomy Dane. 'You are used to such situations, Holmes, whereas I am but a simple play-actor strutting my hour upon the stage and wishing never to become involved with criminal affairs. My visit is really to salve my conscience, I suppose, and to be with those who understand the situation. May I suggest that we perhaps observe a minute of silence for prayer and contemplation when the dreaded hour strikes?'

I shuddered to think what Holmes's reply might be to these pious words but I never gained the chance to find out, for a dramatic intervention took place in the shape of an insinuation of vocal intervention from the street. The newspaper seller called in stentorian tones which we could hear even without raising the window. 'The Long Acre Vampire cheats the gallows . . . murderer slain at the eleventh hour!'

I could not believe what I thought I heard, and Billy was sent to purchase the news sheet which would not habitually form a part of the reading at 221B entitled *The Daily Cryer* and at the time of writing it no longer exists. (Perhaps a reflection of emerging good taste on the part of the reading public or possibly through pressure applied by the establishment.)

Calmly, Sherlock Holmes took up again his task of wrapping and packing, requesting that I should read the pertinent news item aloud. I noticed that the ink was still wet, but I convinced myself as to its validity as Holmes assured me, 'No, Watson, it is not a fake journal. I would scarcely try to use that ruse again. At least, not quite so soon.'

Having therefore decided that the only falsification could be that perpetrated by journalists I started to read:

'LONG ACRE VAMPIRE MURDERER DIES, BRUTALLY SLAIN IN CONDEMNED CELL

'Ritual killing with a stake through his heart, cheats the hangman!

'Only a few short hours before his arranged execution upon the gallows, Robert Jennings, the killer who has been made a legend in his own life-time through his weird vampire-style murders carried out in the Long Acre area, has made a final gory exit. Legend would have us believe that the only way to bring final death and peace to a vampire is through the driving of a stake through its heart. As dawn broke, the prisoner was allowed one last visitor, his brother, George Jennings, who had visited him in prison before without giving cause for concern by the authorities. He was admitted, after his belongings had been carefully checked. The most formidable item that he carried was a walking cane which he evidently needed as was exemplified by his slight limp.'

I stopped reading at this point, catching Sir Henry's eye and raising my brows in question. He at once said, 'I never knew Jennings to limp or indeed to carry a cane in more than twenty years of association. But I suppose he could have suffered a recent accident.' My reading aloud continued:

'Although a guard was present, that official was unable to prevent George Jennings from killing his brother, Robert. He did this in a most bizarre manner and evidently with the full collaboration of the victim. Evidently the cane had been modified by being sharply pointed at its tip; this modification was disguised by a ferrule which, although fitting over this point, could be instantly removed. This done, he had driven the point into Robert Jennings's heart with a thrust that was surprising, given his seemingly modest build.

'There can be little doubt that more details will be available for inclusion in our mid-morning editions.'

I confess that I had read the item with increasing difficulty as I had found the information more and more unbelievable. As for my listeners, Irving had assumed a grey pallor reminiscent of one of the Long Acre murder victims. It was fortunate indeed for him that he was already seated. His voice shook when he broke a silence that Sherlock Holmes had made no attempt to break.

'Great heavens, it is the most dramatic thing I have ever encountered in real life. I suppose Robert induced poor old Jennings to do it to provide fitting finale for the Grand Guignol that he had staged. Mad as a hatter, Holmes, and this proves it.'

176

The detective carefully wrapped the cabinet-framed portrait of Irene Adler as he played out his reply. 'I assume you refer to Robert Jennings when you infer insanity upon the scale of that of the legendary headgear maker? By the way, it is the mercury-based stiffener, or rather the fumes it produces during the hat-making process, that sends them mad, you know!'

Holmes had always, or at least in the time I had known him, had this terrible habit of wishing to clarify the meanings of old adages, even when more important considerations were afoot. But he quickly relented and returned to the main subject. 'Your inference being, my dear Sir Henry, that the raving mad Robert Jennings induced his perfectly sane brother, your dresser, to thrust a stake through his heart in imitation of the exorcism of vampires as suggested by Bram Stoker and dramatized in your play.'

The actor was perhaps no longer quite so certain, having recognized the doubt in Holmes's tone rather than his actual words. 'It is that which first comes to my mind, Holmes. George Jennings is as sane as you and I and this ghoulish action could scarce have been his idea.'

Holmes was sphinx-like of facial expression as he said, 'Come, gentlemen, we must ask Jennings himself about this affair.'

★　★　★

Lestrade greeted us at the prison in a rather crab-like way, saying, 'Didn't take you gentlemen long to hear the tidings, did it?'

Inspector Lestrade had through the years been both help and hindrance to Sherlock Holmes. On this occasion he was more than helpful, for without him we could not possibly have visited George Jennings so soon after the fatal incident.

We found Jennings incredibly calm, and full of resignation regarding his fate. 'Sir Henry, how kind of you to come here to this dreadful place, and Mr Holmes and Dr Watson, I am glad to see you both as well. I am grateful that I have been held in a different place to poor Robert, even allowing for it being in the same building. That condemned cell has an aura of despair.'

Irving spoke words to Jennings which were perhaps as sympathetic and becalming as would have been possible under such horrific circumstances. 'I will do whatever I can for you, my dear Jennings, you know that. I realize that you acted as you felt you had to, supplying a condemned man with his last wish for the *coup de grâce* which he had doubtless implored you for.'

Jennings replied, 'Oh yes, he certainly asked for it!'

Holmes enquired, 'At what point was the promise made to him by yourself?'

'During the trial, for it was obvious what the outcome would be. He is at peace now, and much as I hated the means of his freedom, I prefer it to the thought of his being hanged.'

Holmes decided that he needed to consult with Lestrade, and Irving and I were left with Jennings, although a gaoler was still present. Jennings enquired, 'Sir Henry, do you imagine I will be for the drop?'

The great actor would not hear of this, 'Not if I have anything to do with it, Jennings, for even though you are obviously sound of mind, I believe that the circumstances are extenuating. What do you say, Watson?'

I said, 'Without wishing to raise false hopes, I am inclined to think the same, though I fear that a long prison sentence might be involved.'

Jennings began to unburden himself concerning his early and then more recent experiences with his brother. He explained, 'Robert was always rather strange and as a child he seemed to live in a world of his own. Where other boys might play at being famous explorers or generals, he used to worry the life out of my poor mother when it became obvious that he really believed that he himself was celebrated! Then later his admiration for you as an actor gradually changed, first to his making you his idol and then later still to this deep hatred to which his feelings turned. You know, Sir Henry, it was partly to protect you from his attentions that I first entered your service. Through the years I managed to foil many a plan of his designed to irritate or embarrass you. In this course I largely succeeded until this dreadful Long Acre affair. I didn't know what to do . . . I couldn't turn in my own brother . . . '

He began to shake and sob, so I felt his pulse and tried to calm him. However, at this point there was an interruption in the reappearance of Sherlock Holmes and Inspector Lestrade.

'Come, cheer up, Jennings. You managed to bring about all that you planned, save the finale!'

Irving and I were shocked at his words as well as his brusque manner. He held aloft a small red book. He continued to speak as the actor and I sat motionless, as if hypnotized. 'I have been with the inspector to the condemned cell where Robert Jennings spent his last weeks. He was allowed several concessions as is normal in the case of those condemned to death, and in his case it was mainly concerned with the keeping of a journal.'

He opened the small red volume and began to read aloud: 'They say I am of sound mind and must die, though I rather doubt it, for have I perhaps been driven out of my mind by my brother, George. As boys we got on fine because we both wanted to be actors. But his admiration for Sir Henry Irving got a bit out of hand, though I did think perhaps he had conquered his demons when he went to work for him as a dresser. During those calm years he was evidently biding his time and planning the dreadful actions which he would cause me to do for him; and all because his love for Sir Henry had turned to hate! I suppose I must have been out of my mind when I killed those poor people in Long Acre, but George told me that it had to be done and in the exact manner in which he directed. He said he would see that I was shut in an asylum if I did not do exactly as he said. Then when that nosey Holmes got brought in and had me tried for murder, I felt that to hang me would be fair, for I could not sleep for thinking of what I had done. I think he knows that I have now decided to say something of all this on the gallows. I think they let you have a few words . . . '

At this point Holmes stopped reading from the book and there was a momentary silence. This was broken by Sir Henry Irving. 'Upon my word, Jennings, it was you who caused all this suffering and tragedy through that poor deluded creature. I never would have believed it of you. I was faithfully served by you for so long, I regarded you almost as a friend.'

Jennings spoke, throwing aside that false grief with which he had cloaked himself. 'Almost as a friend . . . you have quite hit the mark with that phrase, Sir Henry. Yes, it is all out now. I planned the killing of those people, and I killed my brother because I feared that he might spout out something at the last minute. I should have realized that he might have written it all down even though he was never much of a diarist. But no jury in the land will agree to try me after I have demonstrated my bizarre actions. I killed my brother when the balance of my mind was disturbed, yes?'

As we left the prison, Sir Henry, shocked but practical, said, 'Be sure you hand the book with the confession to the inspector, Holmes.'

My friend replied, 'I'm afraid no such confession exists. I indulged in a little more play-acting, Sir Henry. But I think that the inspector has heard as much from Jennings as he needs to.'

Lestrade nodded. 'But Jennings was right when he says that he will not be for the drop, or even chokey of the usual kind. He really is a candidate for Haywards Heath, just as his brother should have been. Oh, but Sir Henry is correct in saying that you should hand me that book. After all, it was found in the condemned cell.'

Holmes with due gravity handed the little red volume to the inspector. I leaned over to look more closely at it, and discovered that it was a copy of Bram Stoker's *Dracula*!

As for the trial, this never did take place because a doctor found George Jennings to be insane and therefore unable to stand accused. But he was certified as being a danger to himself and others and was sent to a very secure institution for persons of this kind. Holmes and I had no further connection with him but the good Sir Henry Irving actually visited him at the institution on a number of occasions.

Epilogue

At Simpson's

To the relief of Mrs Hudson, Billy and, I have to admit, myself, Holmes's retirement became postponed through a series of interesting cases which he could not resist taking up. So the brave new twentieth century dawned to find us still at 221B Baker Street. Already I had written the details of the affair involving Sir Henry Irving and had titled it *Holmes's Last Case*, only to soon find that title obsolete, made so by a series of exploits yet to be told.

By the winter of 1903 Sherlock Holmes had packed and unpacked his traps half a dozen times, a process which did not occur other than in a gradual manner, the unpacking largely unintentional. But finally by that time the die had been cast with the transportation of everything, save the bare furnishings, to Sussex. Holmes's violin and a single pipe remained to give the sitting room any sort of character. Every time Mrs Hudson entered at meal times or to announce a caller she was moist of eye and vocally unsure. Holmes, embarrassed by her mournful air, would try and comfort her. 'There now, dear lady, pray do not take on so. Why, soon you will be able to gain a new tenant who will respect your furnishings and keep civilized hours. You will be able to get Hudson to repair the bullet holes in the wall plaster and clean away the chemical stains from the floor and carpets. Just think, life will regain normality for you once you have installed some highly respectable old lady or gentleman in these rooms!'

But his well-meant speeches would invariably produce an effect opposite to that intended and the poor woman would rush sobbing openly from the room, with doubtless the thought of those respectable old bodies having pushed her nearer to the flood of tears.

'Really, Holmes, you are about as diplomatic as the Kaiser!' Although I would chide him I well understood that he was as deeply affected as was his housekeeper at the thought of the upheaval to come.

By this point the reader may well be wondering why I have chosen to marry the affair of Henry Irving with the eve of my friend's retirement, divided as they are by some three years. Well, reason there is and all will be made clear.

By the time of which I write we had not seen or heard from Sir Henry for several years. Therefore, when Mrs Hudson announced him on the particular mid-morning we were quite surprised, though agreeably I should add.

Holmes greeted the famous actor warmly. 'Sir Henry, pray come in and be seated, and I will desire some coffee be brought for you. Dr Watson you know, of course, as well as you do myself.'

The actor made courtly sweeps of his expressive hands. 'Holmes, Watson, my dear fellows, how splendid it is to see you once more. I know you both well enough to realize that you will forgive this unannounced intrusion, especially when I tell you its purpose.'

I poured the steaming coffee and we revelled in its wonderful aroma. Since Holmes's retirement I have never enjoyed coffee as much and indeed have come to suspect that my friend used to give Mrs Hudson some additional ingredient to mix with the ground beans. Certainly I had long noticed that the coffee at 221B appeared to loosen the tongues of our visitors.

The elegant and distinguished actor soon got to the point of his visit. 'My dear Holmes, I just felt that I could not see your impending retirement arrive without being marked in some way. Now I know that you are not a fellow for ceremony, so I suggest that Watson and yourself should join me in a little dinner at Simpson's this evening. Before you say yea or nay, let me add that it will be to mark my own retirement from the theatre as well.'

I had a terrible feeling that Holmes might refuse the kind invitation. But he caught my eye and to my relief he said, 'It will be a pleasure, Sir Henry, although I am far from delighted to hear that you intend to grace the stage no more. No one knows better than I the extent of your talent in that direction. When the part required you to play Sherlock Holmes impersonating yourself I felt that you were skirting the edges of dramatic possibility. Yes, the theatre will be the poorer without you.'

Irving asked, in jovial style, 'Can the great detective deduce the actual reason for my taking such a momentous step?'

Holmes nodded, saying, 'Why yes, Sir Henry, you would not need to tell me the reason for I have deduced that you are having some difficulty with your memory for lines. Further, your eye-sight is not what it should be, and these two infirmities have colluded to force retirement upon you.'

As a medical man I had noticed no symptom of either memory problems nor yet those of vision. But I knew that Holmes would hardly have made such personal observations without being able to substantiate them. The effect of his words upon Irving was far from electric.

'You are right on both counts, Holmes, though how you can know of these impediments, I'm deuced if I know.'

Holmes was looking around him in some confusion. He demanded of me, 'Upon my word, Watson, where have you put my tobacco? Surely you have not packed it . . . I cannot see the Turkish slipper or the jar or any other receptacle.'

I quickly found the tobacco for him in the top of a still open packing case filled with the items that had not been transported to Fowlhaven. I was gently amused that such a great detective could not find his own tobacco, especially given what he was about to reveal. As he filled his pipe he stood with his back to a mantelpiece now denuded of the bric-a-brac that it had trapped in a third of a lifetime. I was saddened to think that this might be the last time that I would see the familiar figure in one of its most typical poses in what was in my mind its natural habitat. He lit the pipe with a vesta which he at least was able to find (the box being in his pocket) and addressed Irving.

'Sir Henry, when we shook hands I noticed some very faint marks upon your shirt cuff. My experience of you in the past has told me that you are fastidious in such matters. I decided that you had been falling back upon an old actor's trick of pencilled cues upon the cuffs as a jog to the memory. No amount of laundering has completely removed that writing.'

The actor examined his cuff. 'Bless my soul, I had no idea that there were still marks upon this cuff!'

'Exactly, which leads me to believe that your eyes are playing tricks with you. Now the actor's trick would lose its use if the eyesight had become unable to benefit from it.'

Sir Henry smiled ruefully. 'You have as usual hit the jolly old nail right on the head. For a while the old actor's trick was a great help to me. But then more recently I just could not see the cues. But then I am an old man and my loss of these faculties is only slight and were I not an actor they would be scarce noticed by myself or others. But you, my dear Holmes, are still a comparatively young man and I notice no loss of cunning upon your part; also I feel sure that you still have eyes like a hawk. You have demonstrated all of this within the past few minutes. Why then have you decided to retire?'

Holmes said, as I knew he would, 'I wish to be remembered as I am at this present time, at the very height of my mental powers and as lean and fit as I was at thirty. If I waited for some sign that these things were no longer true I might mar a career which has been as near perfect as I could make it.'

As for myself, I could say little, having dwelt in a state of semi-retirement for two decades. Sherlock Holmes had not been a man to tell that you could not take off for Dartmoor because you had patients to attend. His retirement would mean that I would need to rebuild a practice which had been so badly neglected.

★ ★ ★

After quite a bit of searching Billy found a hansom to take us to the Strand. (Five years earlier he would have needed to search as long and hard to find a motor taxicab!) We were the first to arrive at Simpson's and awaited the arrival of Irving. To our surprise he was not alone but had a tall, burly companion in the shape of Inspector George Lestrade of Scotland Yard.

Holmes nodded. 'Inspector, our little gathering would hardly be complete without you. Good of you, Irving, to bring Lestrade to help celebrate the retirement of Sherlock Holmes.'

Lestrade was somewhat taken aback by these words and said, 'Sir Henry Irving was kind enough to invite me to take dinner with him to celebrate my retirement from Scotland Yard! I was about to say 'thank you, Mr Holmes' for providing me with a surprise by coming along and bringing Dr Watson.'

The meal was excellent and so was the champagne, with which several toasts were drunk. Irving proposed a toast to Sherlock Holmes who responded and then proposed a toast to Inspector Lestrade. The inspector toasted Sir Henry who unexpectedly proposed my own health. There threatened to be a lull and although I had not expected to make a speech, I found myself standing with my glass held high and saying, 'Sir Henry, and gentlemen, I am honoured to be present to mark the retirement from public life of three such distinguished men. Two detectives and an actor: not by the way the title of a new music hall song.' (Polite laughter.) 'First, Inspector George Lestrade, late of that greatest of all national detective forces, Scotland Yard. I was witness to the first meeting between Lestrade and Sherlock Holmes, and their very first collaboration. The two were as unalike as chalk and cheese, save in their shared ambition to solve crime and bring wrongdoers to justice. Lestrade so determined to follow the policeman's code, Holmes with a mind so open as to accept any possibility or use of his many talents to solve the mystery. Scientist, scholar, musician, boxer, expert with foil and epée, and with a mastery of anagrams, cryptograms and mathematical enigmas. He would use any or all of these talents to discover the guilty thief or murderer, but he needed the support of the solid bulldog that was Inspector Lestrade.

'As for Sir Henry Irving, of his half a

century as Britain's foremost actor/manager, what can be spoken that has not already been uttered by those more theatrically literate than my poor self? Our paths crossed, all four of us, and I was treated to the sheer joy of knowing the great actor far more intimately than would be possible for his mere admirers.'

At this point I made a very great mistake by quoting from the Scottish drama, to the effect that a certain trio might never have the pleasure of again meeting as presently. Irving gasped, and I realized that I had broken some sort of theatrical code. I was made to leave Simpson's, twirl around three times to the amazement of passers-by, and suffered the indignity of pleading with the head waiter for permission to re-enter. Only those who know the superstition will understand this completely, and only those of the theatre can believe how seriously it is all taken.

Of course I do not attach any belief to these old superstitions so as a man of science I have to tell myself that it is pure coincidence that within eighteen months Sir Henry was in his grave, Lestrade had broken his arm whilst pruning an apple tree in his garden and Sherlock Holmes had been badly stung by a swarm of his own bees!

SHERLOCK HOLMES AND THE
BAKER STREET DOZEN

SHERLOCK HOLMES AND THE
SECRET SEVEN

We do hope that you have enjoyed reading this large print book.

Did you know that all of our titles are available for purchase?

We publish a wide range of high quality large print books including:
Romances, Mysteries, Classics
General Fiction
Non Fiction and Westerns

Special interest titles available in large print are:
The Little Oxford Dictionary
Music Book, Song Book
Hymn Book, Service Book

Also available from us courtesy of Oxford University Press:
Young Readers' Dictionary
(large print edition)
Young Readers' Thesaurus
(large print edition)

For further information or a free brochure, please contact us at:
Ulverscroft Large Print Books Ltd.,
The Green, Bradgate Road, Anstey,
Leicester, LE7 7FU, England.
Tel: (00 44) **0116 236 4325**
Fax: (00 44) **0116 234 0205**

DEATH SQUAD

Basil Copper

Lost in a fog on National Forest terrain, Mike Faraday, the laconic L.A. private investigator, hears shots. A dying man staggers out of the bushes. Paul Dorn, a brilliant criminal lawyer, is quite dead when Mike gets to him. So how could he be killed again in a police shoot-out in L.A. the same night? The terrifying mystery into which Faraday is plunged convinces him that a police death squad is involved. The problem is solved only in the final, lethal shoot-out.